T0062765

WORKS IN PROGRESS:

Penelope
In the Shadow of the Barbarian
The Oresteia: Revisited
The Nature of Love: A Metaphysical Journey
Farewell to Philosophy
Dialogues with Friedrich Nietzsche

PENELOPE

AND
ULYSSES

A Journey into the Deepest and Most Longing Love
between Man and Woman

"You should be the guardians of each other's solitude."
~ Rainer Maria Rilke

ZENOVIA
ART BY ZENOVIA

BALBOA.PRESS
A DIVISION OF HAY HOUSE

Balboa Press books may be ordered through booksellers or by contacting:

Balboa Press
A Division of Hay House
1663 Liberty Drive
Bloomington, IN 47403
www.balboapress.com.au
AU TFN: 1 800 844 925 (Toll Free inside Australia)
AU Local: (02) 8310 7086 (+61 2 8310 7086 from outside Australia)

Because of the dynamic nature of the Internet, any web addresses or links contained in this book may have changed since publication and may no longer be valid. The views expressed in this work are solely those of the author and do not necessarily reflect the views of the publisher, and the publisher hereby disclaims any responsibility for them.

The author of this book does not dispense medical advice or prescribe the use of any technique as a form of treatment for physical, emotional, or medical problems without the advice of a physician, either directly or indirectly. The intent of the author is only to offer information of a general nature to help you in your quest for emotional and spiritual well-being. In the event you use any of the information in this book for yourself, which is your constitutional right, the author and the publisher assume no responsibility for your actions.

Any people depicted in stock imagery provided by Thinkstock are models, and such images are being used for illustrative purposes only. Certain stock imagery © Thinkstock.

Print information available on the last page.

ISBN: 978-1-4525-0647-0 (sc)
ISBN: 978-1-4525-0648-7 (e)

Balboa Press rev. date: 01/26/2023

CONTENTS

THE DESPAIR AND LAUGHTER
OF MY THREE MUSES

To my three muses that have lived with me all my adult life and who continue to challenge and inspire me.

To my first emotional and spiritual mother, Amalia, who taught me the wilderness of imagination and the endurance of the human spirit in great stress and conflict. As a young child I sat by the open fire on an empty stomach and listened as my illiterate peasant grandmother exposed me to worlds of both the living and the dead: she spoke of these two worlds as if they lived side by side, and at times she would tell me that all these worlds, in the person and outside the person, co-exist in tension and have a deep longing for each other, "because everything is in love in the world."

At that time I though she captivated my small senses with stories so that I would not feel the hunger, but now I know and I realise "that man cannot live by bread alone."[1] She was preparing me for my emotional and spiritual journey on this tragic but also beautiful planet.

Amalia was training and preparing me for life and how to deal with the crises and conflicts that life brings to all; she was training me to make the choices that were of my true nature and to follow my path, no matter how difficult it got at times. She was training me with great affection, with her stories that breathed and spoke of the true facts of life, the ownership of the self.

It was much later, when I was studying philosophy, that I discovered Plato also said, "The world moves because everything is in love" and that the greatest gift a person can give to themselves and others is to have his true autonomy, purpose, and meaning. Amalia taught me in our solitude and poverty that your character is born and discovered through your actions, through every change, catastrophe and challenge that life and others bring or take from you. She spoke with determination and affection when she advised me "not to fear my life" but rather to take ownership of my nature and destiny. For Amalia not to have lived her life by her true design, by her heart, and her chosen path, was the same as if not being born at all.

How did my grandmother know this? She did not know of Plato's existence, she had not read the great thinkers of our civilisation, she certainly had never read a book in her long life, as she had not gone to school.

I remember the first day at school when I was actually given paper and pencil and was being taught the alphabet. I remember her telling me, "When these people teach you to read and write, don't you get lost in any nonsense that does not smell of life and people. Use what you learn to give life, not divide life, for they tell me that some educated people are very clever and sophisticated, and I do not want you to be clever or sophisticated. I desire you to be in your life and to follow your true path."

As a child I did not understand my need to feel safe and protected, and yet all that she lived and taught me I put inside of me. When she was no longer with me in physical presence I ate from the seeds she planted in my heart, in my soul, in my search among fallen demons and tormented souls.

I remember one day when I was feeling rather small and insignificant in the scheme of things and wanted to know of my importance in her life and if she loved me more than the others. Amalia explained to me my importance in her life, but not in the usual way of saying, "I love you." She used the example of her hand and fingers to show me my importance to her and her life.

"You see my hand and all the fingers attached to it? Because you are so small, you are the smallest finger on my hand. Now, what if I cut my little finger, or my little finger got hurt, would not my whole hand be in pain? So you see, you are as important as the fingers that do most of the work. You are part of my hand, part of my body, part of my life, part of my soul, part of my blood, part of all that moves and breaths in my past, present, and future."

In later years, away from her and away from the island, while I was at university studying philosophy, I read that Plato also refers to a harmonious and caring society as a hand; if one of the fingers gets hurt, the whole hand would know of that hurt. I thank her and her electric memory which is alive in me, in all the things that life brings to me, and all the things that give me challenge, joy, and inspiration.

I still see her sitting in my writing space and smiling and shaking her head as she looks at the symbols that we call writing, as she finds me buried behind books and papers, where I travel into the world of the maker, the inventor, the child, through the exploration of the self, through writing to remain true to my nature, choices, and destiny—"amour fati."[2] Writing is a way back into yourself, and outward to the world—to share your world with others so that "we can speak to each other and understand each other."[3]

I still hear her telling me: "People are going to laugh at you for your ideas and incorrect ways but you must continue on your path and with your incorrect ways or you will die if you don't." One must remain vigilant, devoted and uncompromising to their inner voice, their original and authentic creative self, and the path that belongs to them and them alone. Kafka has such a story in "The Parable of the Doorkeeper" one must go through and into their life—they cannot wait to be given permission to live their lives—to do otherwise, one lives out their life in great despair.

Michelangelo writes that "I must find life where others find death."

The truth of the matter is: if it wasn't for Amalia I would not be alive. I found this planet and its ways alien to me—so many tribes and so many divisions, so many wanting to take parts of your being, so many telling you that their truth is the only truth, so much imprisoning of the human spirit, so much pain and so much indifference, and if I by some chance survived, I would not be in my life as I am but as a sleepwalker. Amalia has stories about the sleepwalkers and she believed that they were neither alive nor dead.

Amalia was what we call my "enlightened witness."[4] She gave me enough emotional and spiritual sustenance that when the world separated us and I was sent to the other side of the world—with a different group of people in a different culture, a different tribe—I had enough of the seeds of love that she had implanted in my heart and soul to feed on, and found and still find myself in the gifts and miracle that was my childhood with my first story teller.

As a child of six, I would listen to the stories she would tell from her life, from her world—stories she had not read in books, stories that contained both destruction and healing—and I would look forward to our evenings together to listen to the stories of man. She was the equivalent to Homer, passing verbal knowledge and history that had been passed on to her from previous generations caught in the human struggle (both in the bowels of the earth and in the sky), the lessons and the decisions made in the challenges of our human condition.

Some of her stories did not have happy endings. They were not based on ego gratification and entitlement but rather on man's struggle to learn and evolve within the design and scheme of life. I realised at an early age that life does not have a plot and we do not control it. The only thing that we do have power over is the way we respond to the changes and conflicts life brings. Sometimes we do not get what we want, and therefore the delusionary happy ending does not come into real life. Instead, we are asked to struggle and endure with a full heart, a heart without resentment and entitlement, the most humane and compassionate lessons that are discovered only in the battle of self-ownership. Therefore, her stories were not based on ego gratification and self-importance in a love affair, rather they were based with being the servant and master of truth and compassion. While other children in different parts of the world would be tucked in bed with a fairy tale that ended with the princess being taken care of by a prince, my bedtime stories ended with lessons of struggle and endurance. Amalia continued to tell me "life will give you impossible tasks, and you will have to make decisions that go against the beliefs of others, you will have to discover life where others find death."

Amalia allowed and encouraged me to wander into the remote wilderness of the forests and learn so many things that one does not learn in a confined classroom. She taught me in her stories about the lamb and the wolf, the hunted and the hunter, the slave and the master, to be neither of each one. She taught me a reverence and worship of life and all that lives here. "You must be careful not to break anyone when you are making decisions. Remain true to your nature. Don't take what is not yours. Do not fear anyone."

In those first eight years of my life I did not know what she was offering me, and now I realise that my illiterate grandmother was voicing the pre-Socratic values and way of life and she gave me the gift of undying protection and undying love.

I thank you, Amalia, for waiting for me.

I thank her for teaching me.

My other friend and intellectual mother was Eleni Kazantzakis. She entered my life at the precious time, the right time, in which I was being hunted for being a writer, in which I was mocked for my creativity, at a time that I found myself totally alone. Eleni Kazantzakis corresponded with me for over twenty years, offering me support and telling me that I would find it very difficult because I was a poet. She advised me that I was struggling in the sea of life because I was a poet, and to continue, continue, continue.

I found her writing to me like a rope that assisted me to get across the difficult bridge that I was building; she would also write and tell me how Nikos Kazantzakis would be concerned about me, as the world hurts the sensitive and our poets. I felt accepted by her, and it was important for me to be accepted and understood by someone academically trained, who had read all the authors that I had found through my love affair with searching and learning from our ancestors. Since I am a "citizen of the world,"[5] these teachers and writers lived in all parts of the world, in different generations. You can't learn about humankind if you only focus on your own kind.

I dedicate this work to her memory: a memory that is electric and alive in me. Eleni assisted me finding my Greek origins, not because I belong to any nation, but I do belong to a group of people that have assisted me in my journey here, and these are the people that she introduced me to once again—my ancestors—for is not a poet a foreigner in his own land?

Eleni told me she would meet me in Constantinople so that I could search for my ancestors.

I never returned to Constantinople because I never left it.

We are carriers of other people; like the layers of our physical earth we also are layered in knowledge and memory. We carry in us our ancestors, those we have met and those we have not met, our teachers that do not belong to our tribe, but to all humankind, our children, both physical, and those we make from our journey and struggles, and put on paper, in music, on canvas. We carry in us all the people we have met and shared life with; we remember their challenges and lessons. Sometimes we are like large haunted houses with so many voices and images, messages, and lessons. We carry all these people in our life. Plato might be right when he says, "nothing dies," it simply goes inward, transforms, and adds to our character. Therefore, I have not felt I needed to see a place to be with them, to have them live in me.

One time I was asked if I have returned to Samos, the island I spent my first eight years of life. I have not returned because the island lives in me; I've swallowed the island, the village, the place, time and child. We have not been parted.

What did your Ulysses write for his epitaph, Eleni?

> I hope for nothing.
> I fear no one.
> I am free.[6]

I thank you, Eleni, for waiting for me.

I thank her for teaching me.

My other emotional and intellectual teacher has been Friedrich Nietzsche. He was a highly educated man, and yet he still wrote, lived, and spoke in the "blood,"[7] the truth of his life, and of course he was influenced by the world that my grandmother spoke about in her illiterate manners and ways. I discovered Nietzsche when I was twenty-four and he has not left my writing space. He guided me to the pre-Socratic philosophers and so many other thinkers. He was more alive in his thinking than the actual university lecturer who tried to understand what he had not lived or experienced with his blood. As Kierkegaard once wrote,

> When I am dead there will be something for the university lecturers to poke into. The abject scoundrels. And yet. What's the use, what's the use? Even though this be printed and read again and again, the lecturers will still make a profit out of me, teach about me, maybe adding a comment like this: "The peculiar thing about this is that it cannot be taught."[8]

Nietzsche taught me to remain true to my blood and to follow my nature and destiny. Even though he has been dead for over a hundred years, his thoughts and journey are alive to me, or as T. S. Eliot wrote, "the dead make more sense than the living."

I am so glad I went into that second-hand book shop and I was drawn to his book. These are the bread crumbs of the soul that others leave for us to find. We have not met them, and yet they are and become kindred and family to us. Nietzsche also believed that his family were the thinkers he had studied and wrote about. Therefore, without knowing of my existence, he offered freely to me knowledge and the seeds from another generation, another time, another world—the seeds of this world as it makes itself over and over again.

It is true what Amalia believed: the living and the dead are in tension and co-exist through deep longing to offer each other love and life.

I thank you, Nietzsche, for waiting for me.

I thank him for teaching me.

All my three great influences and blood loves are dead, and yet there is something so strong in their physical absence, so haunting and lasting: the anchor of their memory, the anchor of their love, the anchor of courage and hope—for hope without courage is only a paper flower (so Amalia thought and wrote in my heart).

It is this living memory that gives life to those who are no longer with us. But first they would have had to be truly alive, and not just in body (millions are alive in body and when they die they are not remembered). It is something more than just physical, although their work is created from the physical.

What makes their memory electric and alive is their passions, desires, and authentic ways, the sacrifices they made for us to get their message, even if they sent it in a bottle. This is what makes my three muses alive in my life and world.

They had the courage to leave some shape or form of themselves, the important part of themselves, the seeds from their soul, the nakedness of their inner world, in literature and in their way of life. They left breadcrumbs of their struggle, their authentic nature, the choices they made that went against the belief and opinions of many, and the hope that their love will keep someone in a different generation, a different time or place, warm and sane.

I am truly grateful to my three muses for allowing me to see the nakedness of their soul, for confining their soul in words or on paper (T. S. Eliot wrote, "When I am formulated . . . how should I begin?"[9]), for making themselves vulnerable and deeply inspirational to me in the darkest night of my creativity and soul.

I thank them for waiting for me.

I thank you for reading this and sharing this journey with me.

All that has been written is from

Myth
Fact
And Nonsense.

INTRODUCTION

The Jewel of Ideals and Despair

The physical earth keeps particles of light compressed for millions of years in total darkness and then this jewel that was created from great pressure and aloneness, separated from all other light particles, surfaces—and what brilliance, what transparency we see in this rare solitaire!

Such is the crisis of the soul in its darkest and most critical night, which is not twenty-four hours but eternity, for numbers do not stop; they go on and on forever.

The Jewel of the Soul is the birth of transparent brilliance in which all faces of life look into the light contained within and see their real face. And how much truth can you bear?

In our history, we have pushed our rarest teachers and masters into the ground. We have wanted to cover the brilliance of their souls. And when we have driven them into the ground, we find we cannot live in total darkness; we cannot live without love.

Like orphans and abandoned people we seek and search the four compasses of our world to see, to find, to seek forgiveness, and to return the brilliance of their souls in a world that has gone mad with either pain or indifference. As people we need the fire, the light of love.

Such a small light contained within, but what turbulence and demanding presence it has upon others who want to bury it again in the earth! The creators of love contain such ideals and despair and reveal and share such a light from the night of the soul. This night has no division of time: it is from the fire of all forming stars. Look closely at "Starry Night" by Vincent van Gogh and you will see the many suns that burned in his exile and on the canvas of his soul. When you listen to Ludwig Beethoven, you are transported into the intimacy of desire, his "rage against the dying of the light,"[10] his deep longing to share his soul and music with us. He believed that music could change the world. He contained "truth and beauty,"[11] and yet he lived in total silence and exile. Is it silence and exile (or solitude) that feeds our desire and longing to create, to invent, to explore, to play above and below the taught rules and dogmas? Even Galileo wrote his most evolved work when he was under house arrest. It is at these times that one refuses defeat, surrender, and nihilism. Instead, one defies without a violent revolution and keeps true to their authentic self and design, which creates beauty and truth in the expression of their life.

I have been in exile and have been writing in my heart, in my head, on the sand, in the sky, and on the tail of the mermaid, long before the world taught me language, long before the world gave me permission to breathe and dance.

For many eons I did not wish to speak with anyone. I had realised that I had fallen into hell. Look at the world through the eyes of our troubled children and you will see the deadness or the rage. Look at Don McCullin's photography and you will see that we have made a hell out of a heaven.

I was driven and separated from the "memory" of another home.[12] As I witnessed injustices small and large, I kept the memory of love alive. This is not how we behave where I come from. I first thought this when I encountered my first injustice when a girl was being mocked because of her deformity, and I could not, and would not, join in. It was as if I had a memory from another home, that we did not behave like this. In later life, when I read Plato, I understood about this former home and this former memory of the good. Where does love come from? Why do some of us carry it? And why do some of us relinquish the right to live in love and then proceed to remove that human right from others? Such a memory of the good requires solitude and devotion to one's life, and to their purpose and meaning in this life. One learns and discovers many untouched and unnamed galaxies in this solitude, and the time has come that I return from exile to surrender to others what belongs to them, to offer to others what was left with me for safe keeping. What I found in my exile, in presence and absence, is deep love for our world. My "art" is my way of living; my creativity breathes and tastes of deep humanity.

At the age of twenty-three I whispered the word "flight" and disappeared into the exile of wilderness and solitude. For ten years I measured the depth and sides of the dark abyss, and in my mad dance I decided to call the abyss my sandpit of forming stars. I could see the stars and I built castles and stairs and climbed into a deeper wilderness and forest of imagination and deep vision.

I fell in love.

I fell in love with the beauty and tragedy of this world.

My next twenty years were spent searching and seeking, of swimming in uncharted and unmapped waters and travelling the roads of chosen solitude and exile.

I have decided to return from my exile.

I decided to return because I desire to devote my creativity to the "young and tender,"[13] as the previous generations have left their questions and the nakedness of their lives to be explored to find a way to each other, to find a way to evolve and enrich our lives so that we do not live in fear and that we are fully in our lives.

I thank the earth for waiting for me. I thank you for waiting for me.

I have struggled to bring this to you, for I am painfully shy and do not seek the attention or recognition of the world. This work is a gift to all our ancestors who have stayed awake at the wheel to navigate our human journey.

This work is a gift of love to all that have passed before me, those that are with me, and those that will find me later.

I am a "citizen of the world,"[14] and at the expense of sounding ridiculous in the world of relativity and appearance, I am a lover of the world and the many worlds that live and breathe in others.

"If we want the Sun to return
we have much work to do,
much struggling as a united people."[15]

The Fire Maker

Of all the fires of the heart, love is the only inexhaustible one.

I am a shy, backward, and awkward writer of myth, fact, and nonsense, and I find it impossible at times to write what I sense in the stream of collective imagination and in the stream of our soul and our humanity.

I find it almost impossible, because I fear attention and the confinement of what is from the profound, sublime, absurd, and ridiculous. To take the risk of baring your soul for all the world to see and judge is both dangerous and ridiculous, but this is the marking and habit of the Lover for life, who is both determined and deeply tender.

There are many who have left their mark on my mind, heart, and body, but there is only one I have always sought and followed: the laws and dark passages of my wandering and seeking psyche.

I am accountable and responsible only to the ways of love. I wrote this for my teachers and mentors who left their blood affirmation for me and others, for those who seek and love my incorrect ways in the moment, and for those who may seek another voice in the song of making, weaving, struggling and creating—the world of the Lover.

The lessons of war are that "we must fight, not in the hope of winning but to keep something alive"[16], to keep love alive.

"I am consumed by a deep longing to find my way home, therefore I know of Ulysses's wandering and searching. I know of his tricksters and phantoms, including the Siren. He was tricked and delayed because she knew the secret of his heart."[17]

I have been consumed by Penelope's plotting and planning to remain true to my nature, choices, and destiny, which is usually, if not always, in conflict with the opinion and direction of the organised might of the barbarian ("men with hearts of stone"[18]) without a heart, without love.

Both of these archetypes have travelled with me, along with the teaching that in order for one to remain Alive and In Love (I don't think anyone is fully alive if they are not in love with life and the world), one must learn the ways of Anathema and Athanasia.

CHARACTERS

Penelope	Aged 45, still physically strong and attractive
Young Penelope	Aged 25
Telemachus	Penelope's son, a young man in his 20s
King Agamemnon	Aged 35
Young Ulysses	Aged 30
Ulysses	Aged 50
Agathy	Suitor 1, aged 35, physically strong and attractive, represents might and sexual aggression
Petroculos	Suitor 2, aged 55, an older man, wily and treacherous, represents Sophist argumentation

VOICES

Andromache	Hector's wife
Astynax	Hector's son, aged 10
Siren	Female
Destiny	Male that has Ulysses's face

* The Penelopes also become The Chorus (Classical Greek theatre).

I chose to have the young Penelope and the older Penelope addressing us in this way not because there is a division in their entity but because there is unison.

How many times have we looked back into our past and seen, and even *addressed*, our decisions? To be able to see the young and older Penelope speaking and answering questions together creates a visual intensity and unison of all her life.

For those that will read the dialogues of *Penelope and Ulysses* before they are set to stage, I will describe the rooms they are in so that you can see and know where these dialogues occur.

During the play we see young Penelope and the older Penelope coming to terms with the decisions and outcomes in her life. Young Penelope brings youth and freshness, playfulness and sexuality; the older Penelope brings wisdom and strength, seduction and determination in fulfilling her journey in life and her purpose in sharing her journey with the audience. Both are physically strong, tender, and accomplished. They project a striking appearance and presence.

Set

The play and dialogues are in two main areas of Penelope and Ulysses' world, which consists of conflict and resolution: the chambers and the seashore. The only exception to this is Agamemnon's scene, in a cold room outside the chambers.

The first main area is the chambers of Penelope and Ulysses. This is the sacred area both share, and later in the play and dialogues, Penelope hides her son in the chamber.

In this chamber is a living tree. Ulysses has built this room around a very old and large tree. Their bed is under the tree, and Ulysses has carved forest scenes into the tree above their heads: this is their secret, since no one else has been in the sacred space together to see what Ulysses has carved in the wood, in the tree for Penelope.

This tree represents The Tree of Life.

The second main area of life and importance, to both Penelope and Ulysses, is the sea. It is the sea that brings Agamemnon to their home. The sea that separates them. The sea that returns Ulysses to Penelope. The sea that she looks at from her window. The sea that she talks to. The sea is the symbol for uncharted and unmapped life.

"There is the sea and who will drink it dry?"[19]

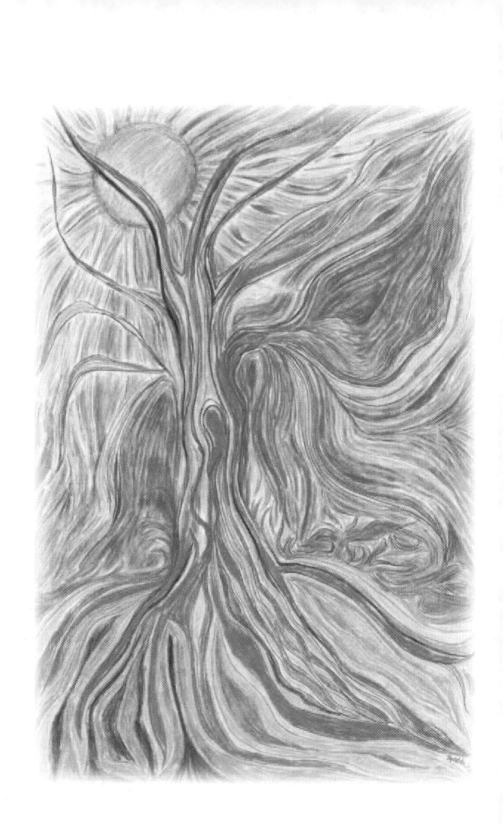

The play is dedicated with deep agape to those
who deeply long to find their home.

PENELOPE and ULYSSES

"I cannot tell the difference between Ulysses and Penelope
for both are navigators and influence the hearts of men."

ACT I

THE ARRIVAL

Colours of Night

'Exerte erthe apo to skotathi'
You have arrived from darkness

[PENELOPE *is a tall, strong woman with long auburn hair. A very attractive woman in both her youth and older age, the* YOUNG PENELOPE *and the older* PENELOPE. *Her face has character, and she has a piercing gaze that makes most feel exposed. She trains for physical battle daily in her chambers, and therefore she is a disciplined warrior in her own right, although she does not share this with others (your best strength is your best kept secret). She does not flaunt her skill with the sword or her head for politics.*

PENELOPE *is dressed in warrior's clothing. Her top is leather with binding and buckles to represent her training and discipline. She refuses to forget herself in woman's comfort and co-dependence, and her clothes reveal her as both feminine and a warrior. The bottom of her skirt is long and sheer, revealing her sensuality and femininity. Her long auburn hair and light green eyes give her the appearance of a seductress, a siren. She wears boots and Ulysses's war bracelets.*

1

We find PENELOPE in her chambers, looking into her youth, bringing to life her youth, and the older Penelope in unison with her youth takes the audience through the beginning of her journey.

Music is heard. 'Dance for Man' (Nikos Xylouris) is played while the audience is settling into their seats. Projected images of Penelope and Ulysses, The Tree, and the sea are seen in conjunction with the music.

Lights slowly come on. They are soft and dark blue. The set is in soft night colours with a gentle mist.

PENELOPE and YOUNG PENELOPE are both facing the audience, looking directly into the distance, into the audience. PENELOPE holds her sword facing downward. YOUNG PENELOPE stands beside her. She speaks the first two lines in Greek—in the language of lost and found worlds.]

PENELOPE: [*Moves forward and addresses the audience.*]
    Exerte erthe apo to skotathi.
    Exerte erthe apo to skotathi. [*You have come from the darkness.*]

[*YOUNG PENELOPE moves two steps forward to stand by PENELOPE.*]

YOUNG PENELOPE: You have come from darkness
    to take parts of my life, to make it yours.

PENELOPE: You have come to recognise or retrieve
    something that you have forgotten or lost.

YOUNG PENELOPE: You have come to see if love exists.

PENELOPE: Oh, by that I don't mean
    comfortable, *grey*, domesticated love.

YOUNG PENELOPE: I mean love that can break and shatter you
    on the rocks of solitude.

BOTH: How much solitude can you bear?

PENELOPE: You have arrived at the precise time of my departure.

YOUNG PENELOPE: Ulysses, Ulysses!
  Haunt me. Drive me mad with longing.

PENELOPE: I want to leave with you the despair and joy—

YOUNG PENELOPE: of a longing and searching,
  of this love for this man—

PENELOPE: for no other man will do.

YOUNG PENELOPE: This love for an ideal,
  this rebellious spark in my soul.

PENELOPE: This love that will not compromise

BOTH: The impossible choices of my nature and destiny.

YOUNG PENELOPE: Will you stay? Give me your hand
  or at least your little finger.

PENELOPE: Please stay, so that I can pass on
  the sirens' song.

YOUNG PENELOPE: Did you know that sirens are mute?
  It is their silence and solitude
  that pierce the heart of your hidden world.

PENELOPE: You all know that the sirens' song
  is the opening of a man's heart
  to reveal either its fullness or emptiness.
  And how much truth can you bear?

YOUNG PENELOPE: Do I have something that belongs to you?
  Others seem to think that I have
  something that belongs to them.

  I have been kept under house arrest
  by those who think that I have
  something that belongs to them.

PENELOPE: Those men in my courtyard are not of my desire,
　　　　of my passion, of my deep sensuality.
　　　　They lack the salt of the sea in them.
　　　　They are not fish, only nets.

　　　　Their lives, their masculinity,
　　　　are nets used to capture the wild bird, the siren.
　　　　They would even settle for the tail of the mermaid.

　　　　They think I watch their nakedness,
　　　　while all the while I look beyond them
　　　　into the waves and turbulence
　　　　of the forever making and breaking sea.

YOUNG PENELOPE: I look to hear Ulysses.

PENELOPE: I search for the sirens

BOTH: Who have escaped the net of the hunter.

YOUNG PENELOPE: I follow the sea with my heart.

PENELOPE: Have you brought the danger
　　　　and beauty of the sea?

YOUNG PENELOPE: Once I found a bottle with a note
　　　　floating in the shallow waters
　　　　of another shipwrecked and sunken world.

BOTH: "There is the sea, and who will drink it dry?"[20]

YOUNG PENELOPE: Ulysses, when we were young
　　　　you felt that I would drown
　　　　because I swam in the unmapped
　　　　and uncharted waters.

PENELOPE: I told you: in these waters
　　　　they do not throw nets.
　　　　You told me there are other dangers.

BOTH: The sea can seduce you and keep you.

PENELOPE: The sea has kept you from me.
    Who can convince the sea to be reasonable?

YOUNG PENELOPE: We are like the bird and fish
    that have fallen in love.
    But where do we live?
    In the sky? In the sea?

PENELOPE: Who would want to tame
    the passion and desire
    of the forever making and breaking sea?

YOUNG PENELOPE: I came from behind the sea,
    and now where do I go
    when it cuts me off?

PENELOPE: Do I want you to stay?
    I can see you, smell you, sense you,
    but something is preventing me
    from touching you.

BOTH: We cannot touch,
    I long for your touch. [*They touch their breasts.*]

PENELOPE: We cannot touch
    because we both are suspended . . .

YOUNG PENELOPE: Above or below our life together . . .

PENELOPE: But we cannot thread our lives
    into the eye of time,
    into the eye of the needle . . .

BOTH: That pierces the heart . . .

PENELOPE: And heat of the moment.

YOUNG PENELOPE: I know a lot about threads
and how far they stretch
and what happens
when they break and disappear.

PENELOPE: Sometimes you have to undo the tapestry
and start again.
But it is never the same.

YOUNG PENELOPE: Something has changed.

PENELOPE: Something is missing.

BOTH: Something is longing.

PENELOPE: What is missing is only the golden threads
that hook themselves into the human heart
and pull upon the other,
to an anchored and shared
destination.

It is only those threads that I weave
and spin in my arrivals and departures.
They lodge themselves in the heart.

YOUNG PENELOPE: In this pulling and tension
between what connects and separates us,
the golden thread that will not break
always pulls the anchor in my heart.

PENELOPE: We are both suspended
upon the invisible thread of a time
that does not meet the heat of the physical.

YOUNG PENELOPE: We are suspended like stars.
We watch the light of the other
but we cannot feed from each other's heat.
Who are the philosophers who say
that the physical does not matter?

PENELOPE: I feel everything
    through the longing of my body,
    the longing of my deep rebellion.

BOTH: I am from another world, another time
    that has burned into the fragility
    of the passing moment,
    the moment that has become my eternity.

YOUNG PENELOPE: For I am meant to live
    from the moments I have had with you
    for the rest of my life,
    beyond and further
    than any trained navigator can go.

PENELOPE: Ulysses, you have shipwrecked me
    on an island surrounded by men
    whom I must seduce
    so that I can remain devoted
    and faithful to you,
    so that I keep you alive in me.

YOUNG PENELOPE: How do you seduce a man?

PENELOPE: Through sexual favours?

YOUNG PENELOPE: Through food and comfort?

BOTH: That is not seduction,
    only a temporary need gratification
    that one can get with anyone,
    at any time.

PENELOPE: Seduction of all the senses.
    I know the secrets of the sirens.
    I know how to keep men
    burning and longing.
    I am from the hidden,
    the unknown, the untouched.

YOUNG PENELOPE: For ten years they have lived outside me.
    For ten long years they seek
    my favours and choice
    of one of them.
    At any time they could have and can,
    conquer, and steal what is not theirs.
    Instead they wait for the prize.

PENELOPE: To taste and eat
    from the seed of the seductress
    who is both a bird and a fish.

YOUNG PENELOPE: Aren't you glad that I learned to swim
    in uncharted and unmapped waters
    so that I can live
    on this suspension of time, in longing?
    Aren't you glad that I swim
    in uncharted and unmapped waters,
    the darkest turbulence of my heart,
    so that I can learn the secrets of seduction
    that keep me in love and others desiring me?

PENELOPE: Like you, Ulysses, I am a navigator
    and influence the burning of my vessel
    so that you may see me,
    but others can come and claim this fire.

YOUNG PENELOPE: Like you, Ulysses,
    I seduce the senses of men . . .

PENELOPE: And influence their hearts to follow me . . .

BOTH: In preparation for their arrival and departure.

YOUNG PENELOPE: I am your love,
    and yet I am unattainable
    and absent from you.

PENELOPE: I am from your hidden world,
   from your sunken world,
   from your lost and forgotten ideals,
   from the ashes of your youth,
   from the sparks of your passion and desire.

YOUNG PENELOPE: I am the one you love,
   the one you avoid,
   the one you hide from,
   the one you find too intense . . .

PENELOPE: too demanding,
   too overwhelming
   and yet you will not let me swim past you.

BOTH: Why do you keep me alive
   in the ashes of your unspoken and unfulfilled?

YOUNG PENELOPE: Do you have any idea
   the deep despair and aloneness
   I retreat into
   when I cannot hear your voice,
   see the sea in your eyes,
   feel your heat near me,
   feel your heat on me and in me?

BOTH: I am Penelope the blesséd and curséd.

PENELOPE: In my courtyard
   I have naked men that seek me,
   and I desire and long for the absent,
   the uncharted, the unmapped.

BOTH: I seek the journey of the heart.
   I seek the body and seed of Ulysses.

PENELOPE: And there is my blessing and curse.
   For twenty years I have ached for him,
   longed for him, searched in the sea for him,

asked the sirens about the secrets of his heart.

BOTH: All remain silent.
　　　All remain hidden,
　　　unseen and still.

PENELOPE: Did you hear that?
　　　There it goes again.
　　　The creaking and moaning of a vessel
　　　that has been on the sea for too long.
　　　You all have come from the darkness
　　　to take parts of my life,
　　　to make it yours.
　　　I have travelled into the unmapped
　　　and uncharted worlds
　　　of the searching, the seeking,
　　　the deep longing of the heart.

YOUNG PENELOPE: The unfilled heart.

PENELOPE: The untouched desires.

BOTH: The fires that burn and keep me alive.

PENELOPE: I have waited for you to arrive.
　　　You have arrived at the precise moment
　　　of my departure.

BOTH: Will you stay?

PENELOPE: Will you take me with you when you leave?
　　　Have you been searching
　　　for decades or eons,
　　　an eternity?

BOTH: "There is the sea and who will drink it dry?"[21]

YOUNG PENELOPE: Have you brought
　　　the turbulence of the sea with you,
　　　in you?

PENELOPE: Do I want you to stay?
    I can see you,
    smell you, sense you,
    but something is preventing me
    from touching you.

YOUNG PENELOPE: The physical.
    How I desire the physical.
    Even my teacher Socrates understood
    all experience comes through senses,
    the blood of the physical.

BOTH: For I desire and know
    only what is of earth,
    sea, sky, and man.

PENELOPE: In my tapestry I weave the mighty breakers
    that have shipwrecked me here.

YOUNG PENELOPE: In my tapestry
    the salt of your tears
    and seed can be tasted.

PENELOPE: Do you have the burning desire
    to be consumed by the journey of the navigator
    who seeks the hidden, the unknown?

YOUNG PENELOPE: Do you have the courage
    to swim where mermaids and sirens
    lose their glory?

BOTH: Or is all your journey predictable
    and rewarded by the acceptance of mediocrity?
    Safety and security in the name of love.
    I am afraid to be without you, love.
    What of your Journey?
    The one you were meant to make?
    What of your Journey?

PENELOPE: There it goes again.

[*NOISE: something falling, breaking.*]

YOUNG PENELOPE: Did you hear it?

PENELOPE: Did you see it?

[*Flickering of fire light*]

BOTH: Did you feel it?

ULYSSES [*offstage*]: Penelope!

BOTH: Did you hear it?

PENELOPE: The groaning of a ship
    that has carried too much in deep waters,
    the groaning of my life,
    the ache of the sirens
    that are driven by the tenderness of truth.

ULYSSES [*offstage*]: [*loud*] Penelope! [*soft weeping*]

BOTH: There it goes again.

YOUNG PENELOPE: I can hear him, in me.

PENELOPE: I can see him in me.
    I can hear him in the darkest silence,
    the mutest world.

YOUNG PENELOPE: He is calling for me.

PENELOPE: He is seeking me.

YOUNG PENELOPE: He is thinking of me.

PENELOPE: All the women he loves have my face.
    All have to make this sacrifice to him and me.

YOUNG PENELOPE: All witches, all goddesses
    have to change their face to mine.

PENELOPE: And when they love him
    it is I who collect him to me.
    It is I who receives his gift in me.
    The longing.

[The stage darkens.]

PENELOPE: *[holding his sword above her head, whispers]*
Ulysses! Ulysses! *[offers her sword to YOUNG PENELOPE]*

[Complete darkness.]

Note: At the end of the dialogue when the elder PENELOPE finishes her "longing of Ulysses," the YOUNGER PENELOPE will take the sword from her hand, lift it up, and run into the next Act, which is "Joy."

The lights will go dark and then light up to a sunny beautiful day, with only YOUNG PENELOPE on stage to be followed by YOUNG ULYSSES and the start of Act II.

ACT II
JOY

Colours of Spring

[*Ulysses and the young Penelope are in their sacred chambers, madly in love, but they also sense that something will enter their world that will change them and their world together forever. Nothing will remain the same, and sensing this, they are vividly intense, enjoying every moment they have together. These moments will have to feed them, in the face of adversity, uncertainly separation, or even death. That is why this dialogue between them is so intense and playful.*

The lights work in harmony and together.

As the lights diminish around PENELOPE, the YOUNG PENELOPE will enter the stage and the lights become bright.

YOUNG ULYSSES is dressed as a warrior. He is strong, happy, and in love.

Both YOUNG PENELOPE and YOUNG ULYSSES enter at the same time, YOUNG PENELOPE in front of him and he following her. Bright yellow lights.]

YOUNG PENELOPE: Ulysses, Ulysses.
    You lost your sword to me.
    [*laughs and puts his sword behind her neck.*]

[*Music. PENELOPE starts to dance "The Song of Penelope"—a warrior's dance.*
                    ULYSSES watches and at the ending joins her
              in their play and worshipping of each other's body and youth.]

YOUNG ULYSSES: Once more, my love.

                    [*They swordfight with neither one dominating.*
        Then they bow to each other in mutual respect of each other's skills.
    ULYSSES bows to YOUNG PENELOPE and she returns his sword.

They kneel in front of each other and revere each other's beauty.
They are on their knees facing each other in deep longing and desire.]

I swear by all that makes and breaks me,
my purpose is to always find you,
to always seek you,
to always long and ache for you,
my beloved and desirable lover.
Whatever life, with all its turns and twists,
brings or asks,
by the power of the gods,
the anger of the devils,
the rage of the furies,
and whether I have been blessed in heaven
or cursed in hell; I am in heaven and in hell,
I will worship you every night.
[*puts down his sword and kisses her passionately.*]

YOUNG PENELOPE: And will you not reverence me
in the morning?
For not to be with you
would be for me an eternal night
in which I would stay on the sea of life
searching and seeking and longing for you,
in every passing port,
every passing face.
The earth with all its passing beauty
would be a world of darkness.

YOUNG ULYSSES: Did you know, Penelope,
that before I saw your face
I loved you as a formless shape and flame?
You have haunted me since long
before I knew your name.
When I saw your eyes,
your smile, your face [*touches her face tenderly*],
I knew I was with my woman.

I knew I had the incarnation
of all loving—
you are all women to me.

YOUNG PENELOPE: Did we dream of each other
before we met?
I had already heard your voice
in my dreams.
I recognised you when I heard your voice.
I had come home.
Or was it that you had come home to me?
I arrived and you had waited for me
with kindness and tenderness.
Every moment, every second is to be lived and consumed
in the fire of our love.
You are the fire
in my moment
and the seed from eternity.

YOUNG ULYSSES: Therefore, there is no other way—
I will reverence and delight
in the joy that you bring to me
for I will need to carry
these moments with me
when the sea calls me back to her,
when my destiny takes me away from you.

YOUNG PENELOPE: The sea—she is your mistress
and she surrounds my world.
Why are you listening
to her murmuring?

YOUNG ULYSSES: I do not listen to her murmuring
with my ear.
The murmurs,
sighs, whispers,
and rage are in my heart.

My heart resembles the tides
    and passions of the sea, swirling
    and raging the river of blood in me.
    We are all related to the desires
    and passions of the sea.

    Last night I dreamed
    that the sea was calling me,
    "Ulysses, return to me."

    All her sirens and mermaids
    have your face and voice, Penelope,
    and all were tempting me.

    I struggled to hide from her song
    and all the while my heart beat and raged
    like her mighty breakers.

    My heart never rests.
    It is always moving,
    making, breaking, flowing
    in deep tenderness or dark rage.

    It is always awake.
    Always seeking and longing.
    And all the while,
    her unheard song became louder
    in the echoes of my silence.

YOUNG PENELOPE: My love. We cannot escape the turbulence
    of the forever making and breaking decisions
    of our nature and our destiny.
    We cannot escape the sea.
    She lives inside us and outside us.
    We are floating in her and on her.

YOUNG ULYSSES: The untranslated, unopposed song
    became as intimate to me as my breathing

and I realised that her hands reached out
to touch me.
They were your hands, Penelope.
Your long fingers
and pale, delicate skin [*touches her hair*].
The seaweed had become your hair
that was entangling me
and binding me to her.

YOUNG PENELOPE: "There is the sea and who will drink it dry."[22]

YOUNG ULYSSES: I did not struggle, I did not fight.
I floated to the bottom of her world
only to be tossed and spat out.
I woke to find you sleeping next to me.
I had been thrown and I caught you
in the tree
that we have made our bed.

YOUNG PENELOPE: What do think this means?
Why do you and I continue
to swim where the mermaid
loses her glory?

YOUNG ULYSSES: This is how we are made. By our choices.
The choices that have become
our destiny and journey in life.
And yet, my love,
you have a different destiny from mine.
You are a weaver of the golden threads,
faithful and devoted to finding
the anchor of my threaded heart.
You are devoted to the unwritten laws,
of the golden threads of love.

YOUNG PENELOPE: I am a weaver of dreams,
stars, rivers, mountains
and my home, the tree.

YOUNG ULYSSES: Penelope you are not weak,
    and although you weave dreams
    you are not absent from life,
    like so many women and men
    who seek only the security and safety
    of the known and taught.

    Theirs is domesticated love that prevents them
    from taking the journey into their life
    and into the life of the other.

    My beautiful wild bird and silent siren,
    I fear that the world will not allow us
    to conspire for too long with each other.

YOUNG PENELOPE: Will others come to separate us?

YOUNG ULYSSES: We do not always steer the course
    of our vessel. There are times that the sea of life
    will remove us from all
    that we have known and loved.

    There are times the force and might of others
    crash into our vessel,
    into our life,
    into our world
    and nothing,
    nothing
    remains the same.

YOUNG PENELOPE: The seas and storms of our lives,
    the crises of our lives,
    remove us from what we have known
    as the lighthouse.
    In these crises we either remain devoted
    to this love or to our betrayal
    of all that is life-giving.

YOUNG ULYSSES: I hear many drowning sailors,
      long before the sirens expose the secret
      of their hearts. Their pleading and curses
      can be heard in the winds by all others
      who have not been shipwrecked in their lives.

      Their laments and tears can be heard
      as we sail into the dark waters
      of the crises of our life: the breaking away
      from all that gave us safety and security,

      when the island has been sunk,
      the tree has been cut down,
      and we surrender to all
      that makes and breaks us.

YOUNG PENELOPE: I sense we will be tossed
      and turned inside out.

      YOUNG ULYSSES: Haunted and hunted
      by something that is moving,
      breaking, creeping, and crawling
      towards our shore.

      I can hear the moaning of the sea
      as the burdened and overloaded ships
      creak with the weight of lead and death.

      YOUNG PENELOPE: Nothing will remain the same.
      All will change.

      We will all be scattered
      away from our homes,
      away from our loved ones,
      away from the safety of the light.

YOUNG ULYSSES: I know my time with you,
      I know my time without you.
      I have known you in absence

and now in presence.
And there will come a time
in which I will love you
without touching your body.
I love you in absence, once again.

BOTH: In that absence,
you will become as intimate to me
as my breathing.
[*They breathe into each other's mouth.*]

YOUNG ULYSSES: How does one love
a wild bird that seeks to live
in the heart of a navigator
without domesticating or confining?

YOUNG PENELOPE: Your physical tenderness and softness
reduces me to my knees. [*falls to her knees*]

YOUNG ULYSSES: I fall to my knees and give thanks [*falls to his knees*]
to all that makes and breaks me
for allowing me to experience
the miracle of woman.
My woman!

YOUNG PENELOPE: Come kiss me,
my beautiful and dangerous Ulysses.

YOUNG ULYSSES: I love you with such a youthful passion
that I will be able to taste you on my skin
when I cannot be with you.

YOUNG PENELOPE: No heaven or hell will remove you
from the sea that consumes me,
the sea that brought you to me.

YOUNG ULYSSES: The sea that calls me
and claims me as hers.

YOUNG PENELOPE: The sea that I had to travel to find you.
The sea that will keep me from you,
my love,
my love.

YOUNG ULYSSES: The women I knew before you
all had your face.
All the sirens, witches, and goddesses
who enter my sleeping state
will have to have your face,
your hands, your voice, your breasts, your smell.
I will always see your face
in every woman.

So, tell me my clever wife,
when I started training
and teaching you
how to stand in war,
how to defend yourself,
I did not suspect
that you had mastered the craft of the sword.

YOUNG PENELOPE: Why are you surprised?

YOUNG ULYSSES: And why should I not be surprised?
I have always counted and depended
on your clever and cunning ways
in reaching a destination
without being heard or seen.

I know the answers
as you know my questions.
I suspect that you have been training secretly
not only for the battles of war
but also for the knowledge
of our poets and dancers.

I suspect you are acquainted
with the philosophers.
I believe that you have spoken also
with Pericles's concubine,
the one who so impressed Plato.

YOUNG PENELOPE: Aspesia?

YOUNG ULYSSES: What does the famous Aspesia say about Pericles
and how she seduced
all his senses—all six of them?

Think of this, Penelope.
She would be a woman of your heart.
There was Pericles—married.
Not happily married, but married all the same.
He made laws about the way
other men should live
and how they should
conduct themselves in private and political life.

YOUNG PENELOPE: And just when he had denounced
the lover and fool in the world,
he fell in love, head and all ten toes, with Aspesia.
He paid his friend to seduce
and convince his legal wife
to run away with him
so that he (Pericles) could have a life
with his beloved Aspesia.

YOUNG ULYSSES: Do you think that she also
was a weaver and spinner
of dreams and stars,
and the promise of dawn?

YOUNG PENELOPE: I have come to the conclusion
that very few fall in love, very few can love.
Rather, the fear of being alone

makes them delude themselves
that they are mated for life.

Security, comfort, prestige, acceptance.
Fear, fear, fear, fear.

The fear of being alone.

YOUNG ULYSSES: You, on the other hand, Penelope,
　　　are not afraid of being alone.
　　　You are not afraid to resist,
　　　to plot and plan.
　　　You are a master
　　　with the threads of the heart.
　　　"How I love a clever woman."[23]

YOUNG PENELOPE: The investigation of life:
　　　My place in the world
　　　and the world's place in me.
　　　I do not want to change the world,
　　　but I do not want the world to change me.
　　　How can you say that you are alive, truly alive,
　　　if you do not search and investigate beyond,
　　　above and below the safety
　　　of taught things,
　　　below and above
　　　the safety of mediocrity?

YOUNG ULYSSES: How can you love if you fear?

YOUNG PENELOPE: As for me, my training with the sword
　　　and my discipline in the art of philosophical persuasion
　　　is to protect you and our son.
　　　It is to protect you, my love.

　　　You look surprised!
　　　You of all people should know
　　　that when life sets me a task

I will continue to live in it
until I can master it.

I do not reveal myself
as one of the hunted or the hunters
in moments of danger and war.
Nor do I show my weakness to my enemy.

Therefore, one needs strategy,
purpose, and planning
to avoid the nets of either
the slave or the master.

YOUNG ULYSSES: And what of your dancing feet, Penelope?
Will the hunter follow your tracks
to the Dionysian worship and reverence for life?

YOUNG PENELOPE: It was you who told me about
the unknown philosopher
who searched into
the hidden things of life,
into the seen things of death,
and into the deep longing for the "eternal recurrence,"[24]
the hidden and revealed things of life,
and went mad.

I have seen him dancing
in Dionysian processions.
He is the lover and the fool and he is near.
He had mad dancing feet.
You have to be a dancer
to jump over the abyss.

YOUNG ULYSSES: Is it over the abyss, or into the abyss?

YOUNG PENELOPE: You jump into the abyss.
How else will you know its secrets
and find a way under it or above it?

How else if you do not live in it?
Did he not say that your friend
should have the courage
to be your enemy?

YOUNG ULYSSES: Penelope, do you love me so deeply
that you would risk my anger and rejection
by telling me what I do not want to hear,
what I do not want to face?

Yes, Zarathustra did say
that when you love,
you should have the courage and strength
to expose all parts,
all the unspoken
and all the hidden
to the other.

YOUNG PENELOPE: In our love there is no fear,
no guilt, no shame,
no rations, no compartments,
only reverence and devotion.

YOUNG ULYSSES: This is not an idealistic ideology;
this is a way of life for me.
As a warrior of many battles
and many experiences
in the struggle for life and death,
I have come to realise the world
has gone mad
with either pain or indifference.

Man has lost his way
and struts around in his life,
like a sleepwalker,
and he is not in his life,
and lives out his years
as a shadow of himself.

YOUNG PENELOPE: I could not have the passion and strength I have
    if I did not have the will to endure
    and ask for more.
    I have a deep love for the world
    and my place in it—
    not outside it,
    in it.

YOUNG ULYSSES: You sing to me the song of the sirens,
    for you open my heart
    and reveal the fullness
    that multiplies in truth and beauty,
    and expose the complexity and diversity
    of my choices
    that have brought me to you.

YOUNG PENELOPE: I am your whole,
    your equal, not your half.
    Not your "other half,"
    not the "little woman"
    who will pass with time,
    who will grow grey and vanish
    from your desire and passions,

    who will start as your lover,
    be transformed into wife,
    reduced to sister,
    and finally abandoned
    as a sexless partner.

YOUNG ULYSSES: I would rather leave for foreign shores
    than to place such a yoke
    of convenience and commodity
    upon our love.
    I would leave, denouncing all
    that gives me security and safety
    rather than to face

a loveless union,
a cold body,
and grasping hands.

Did not your mad philosopher also say
that when you stop loving me,
you don't understand me?

YOUNG PENELOPE: Yes, Ulysses, Yes! I want you to burn for me.
For how can you be truly alive
if you do not have a fire in the belly?
I wanted to tell you that I am the warrior
who will be with you in all your battles,
lost or won.
I swear by my sword [*lifts her sword*],

I am your army, Ulysses.
I am the foot soldier you leave behind
to keep the fire burning,
to keep the fire of the lighthouse alive so that you will always find your
way home, back to me.

YOUNG ULYSSES: And who can convince the sea to be reasonable?
Why does it create such strange creatures
like you and I?

Tell me, *agape mou*, if a fish and bird fall in love—
as at times they will and do—
when a bird and fish fall in love,
where do they live?

YOUNG PENELOPE: You and I are like the bird and the fish.
Do we live in the sea or in the sky?
Do we live in each other's heart?
Both of us are bound by our nature and choices—
one feeds the other,
and both of us have a separate destiny.

We meet and love and pledge
in the moments
that we forge with our souls, as our eternity.

Both of us will remain with each other
when these moments
of physical intimacy and discovery
have been removed from us.
In your absence
there is a haunting presence.

YOUNG ULYSSES: Penelope, my love,
we are both navigators
in the sea of the life.
We travel and hide
from all the world,
and yet we are both found.

YOUNG PENELOPE: *Agape mou,*
you are the salt in my bread,
the salt in my tears, the salt in my body.

YOUNG ULYSSES: You consume me and spit me out,
like a fish that flounders.
I cannot live without being in you.
There is no life unless I am swimming in you.

YOUNG PENELOPE: You are a swimmer in life, Ulysses.
In my past I have been in prison,
in confinement, under house arrest.
They even sealed the windows
so that I could not see the sea or sky.

But they could not seal the eyes
of my searching and aching soul.

YOUNG ULYSSES: I did not think that you lived.
I thought that for some reason or other,

men would have hunted you
and netted you,
and you would have died from grief.
For it is true: when you confine a wild bird
it will fret and die from grief.
And you are a wild bird.

YOUNG PENELOPE: I also thought that upon my arrival in your life
you would be bound and bled
and you would have asked me
to travel alone,
alone, alone—

YOUNG ULYSSES: In the sea of life,
you will travel alone.
In the journey of longing
I cannot be separated from you,
as stars cannot be separated from their light,
and all good sailors will tell you,
we are lost on the sea
without the stars to guide us.

YOUNG PENELOPE: Some people say it is better
not to find your other whole
because of the grief and suffering
that is experienced upon physical separation.

I am happy to reach out and accept this price,
to drink of this cup.

And what if I found you bled,
shattered, and broken, Ulysses?

That for me would have been a double death:
first, that the hunters had killed you,
and then your captive sad eyes
would have killed me again.
Does a double death bring about a double life

for a Dionysian dancer,
who has her eyes in her feet?

YOUNG ULYSSES: What a defiant spirit!
What a deep desire I have for you!
No! I burn for you,
in your presence and your absence.

I was convinced that they
would have netted you
for your gifts.

YOUNG PENELOPE: I was promised by my father
to a certain educated barbarian,
who thought that he would break me
by ridiculing and humiliating
my ways of seeing and living in the world.

My father told me that you did not exist.
He told me that I was seeking
a cat with five legs.
He told me that you were dead.

He told me that love does not exist
and only wealth and power
will bring the world to its knees.

I did not want to bring the world to its knees.
I wanted to worship and love another
in all their tragedy and beauty.

I was not allowed to swim or fly,
and I turned inward
to discover the sea and the sky.
At an early age
I was under house arrest,
and my movements
were watched and measured.

I learned to play with threads,
traps, and prisons
so that I could remain,
so that I could continue,
so that I would not surrender
the world that makes and breaks me.

I learned from any early age,
before you pulled me out of the sea,
how to listen without words,
to see what others hide
and where they hide it.

I learned to avoid the hunter and the hunted,
while all the time
I lived in the cave of the hunter.

I had to learn how to remain alive,
in the net of the freshly caught.
I did not compromise
my thoughts, my heart, my body.
I plotted and planned
to find a cut in the net
or a cut in me,
in which I would remain free.

During the day I was obedient
and wore the yoke of the ox and the calf
in obedience.

YOUNG ULYSSES: What did you do during the night,
    my Dionysian weaver and dancer?

YOUNG PENELOPE: During the night,
    I walked on the forbidden path.
    I carved a wing on my right ankle
    so that I could fly lopsided to the mountain
    that contained the treasures

of imagination and vision.

I searched into the eyes
of all who spoke to me.
I listened with my eyes
to see the flicker of your fire,
to see you just once,
just for five minutes.

I would settle for a second
rather than not have you at all.

YOUNG ULYSSES: I want a universe for you
    where nothing dies.
    All the great thinkers,
    of all cultures and generations
    cannot answer
    why anything has to die.

YOUNG PENELOPE: Is there a universe that does not die?

YOUNG ULYSSES: Yes, there is a universe that does not die;
    it simply continues and is passed on,
    generation to generation.
    I am not a poet, Penelope.
    I am a man of war
    and I believe what I see,
    not what I am told by philosophers or poets,
    although I have an affection
    for these sensitive souls.

    What I have seen in the struggle for life,
    in the struggle with death,
    is there is a universe that does not die,
    and that universe is the seed of the human spirit
    in struggle with longing, separation,
    and physical death,
    and the greatest desire and longing

to fly back into the heart of their loved one,
to live inside their loved one,
in their longing and living memory.

This universe does not die;
it simply continues,
impregnating the loved one with longing
and uniting them with the infinite in the finite,
having particles from both worlds
in your memory and soul.

These areas of our human life
with each other,
and without each other,
death cannot dissolve or conquer.
We have experienced them,
we have lived them,
we are of them,
and they cannot be removed by death.

Is a man dead when the living speak of him
as though he is still living?
Is that in the past or in the present,
to be continued in the future?

How can a man be dead
when he is remembered and spoken about
among the living?
Is not the most important part of him
alive in the living?
Has he not transformed into many,
rather than one?

Of course this cannot be done
without the courage and strength
of deep lasting humanity.

Kings come and go,
tyrants come and go,
but the uncompromising love
for one another continues.

It only dies when it is betrayed and compromised,
forgotten, or neglected,
or murdered by the laws and actions
of entitlement over the other.

Strange talk for a soldier.

See how your threads have taken hold,
and they cannot be broken,
these threads to my heart
that I welcome?

PENELOPE: Ulysses, did you hear that?
I can hear something moving towards us.
It is slithering in the grass;
it is coming towards us.
I can hear the chains of the civilised barbarian
travelling towards us.

This barbarism that presents itself
as human and humanitarian.

There is stealing of human life,
and the deception of the spider,
the web that will ensnare so many of us.
The organisers and planners
hunt and kill the heart of the universe,
the heart of the young and innocent,
for accumulation, for domination, for wealth, for power.

ULYSSES: I have come to see and understand
that you can do much to improve
someone without education,

without manners or refinement,
without skills or accomplishments,
a man that is confused,
lost, or even betrayed.

But you cannot do anything,
not a single thing,
with a man who has excessive weakness,
a man who has made choices that are based on weakness,
a man who has chosen the destiny of a pathetic coward

and yet will present himself as a leader among men,

present himself as a
human during the day
while he organises armies
and hunts people during the night.

You cannot teach wisdom to a malignant mind.

YOUNG PENELOPE: You have come to understand
so much about the organised,
democratic barbarian
because you have lived among them:
you were one of them.

I love you, Ulysses,
because I know who you were,
who you are,
how you have used your sophistry and persuasion
in taking armies to foreign shores
and bringing back
what has not belonged to us.

Would I have not been happier
with a piece of bread and water,
would I not been happier
to know that my husband

was not stained with blood?
—"for blood will have blood."[25]

My beloved, my tormented husband,
do those that you have killed
visit you in your sleep?

YOUNG ULYSSES: You are the keeper
of my unspoken torment and grief.
Yes, they do visit me when I sleep
as I know that the living will soon visit me again
and ask me to return to stealing the land
that belongs to others,
stealing and sealing their lives with lead and spear,
fertilizing their land with their blood,
as we cut away generations to be born.

I know these things, Penelope,
because I have been a hunter
and will be a hunter again,
in the accumulation of my lands.

These men of excessive appetites will seek me again.
I am bound to them
by the blood of the men we have killed.
I am wedded to them
by the blood of the men we have killed.
What binds us is not friendship or humanity,
it is the crimes that we have committed,
it is the spilled blood of another.
It is the spilled blood of many.

YOUNG PENELOPE: You have the courage
to face your decisions
and the demons they have brought
into your life and mine.

Your blood friends will separate us
for they separate the moon from the sun.
They call day, night,
and night, day.
They separate, divide, alienate, conquer, and crush
until one goes mad or dies from grief.

YOUNG ULYSSES: They will come.
They will seek my skills
and later, they will seek you.

You must always be ready for your departure;
one must always be in training
for when the hunter throws the net.
Until that time,
surrender to me
what belongs to me,
what is of me and you.

Teach me about tenderness,
about unbroken and unfractured life.

I have sharp senses.
War sharpens your senses and your appetite.
I have become skinless
and feel things quicker,
deeper, and sooner.
War has disturbed my order
and balance of things.

War has made me dangerous to you!
My love, your future decisions
will disappoint many.

YOUNG PENELOPE: I am happy to disappoint those
who seek to use me
for their self-interest and self-gratification.
I will not disappoint or neglect my decisions

that direct and guide me to my destiny.

YOUNG ULYSSES: What is it, my love? You look concerned.

YOUNG PENELOPE: Ulysses, I fear for you,
for your cleverness will draw
your old friends to you
and both your friends and your enemies
will seek you.

Your gifts, your choices, your decisions
will bring the net to Ithaca,
will bring the net
to our lives,
to our world.
They will throw the net
of domination and oppression
over our world
as you have thrown it over your past enemies' lives.

YOUNG ULYSSES: My friends are organised
and methodical, democratic men.
They write the law by day,
and by night they steal and murder
strangers, land, and life.
The ones who eat the children of the enemy
like to present their deeds of horror and death
as actions they had to make
for the good of all—
the progress of the world.
Bad deeds are transformed into a necessity.
Their barbaric murder of the sleeping enemy
is transformed into a humane cause
of democratic, civilised order.

One of my soldiers once said to me,
"A job like this is not for a man
without feeling or decency;

I'm not half brutal enough."[26]

YOUNG PENELOPE: Was it then that you realised
that we are plunging
into the abyss of pain?
They will open the heart of the kindred and the stranger
with hooks and metal tools of torture
to see if they can capture
the lover and the fool.
And then they will want to put in their hand
to remove all the seeds of the future generations.

The more you maim, torture, kill, and burn,
the more rewards they will give you
and make you even more famous and wealthy.
The more you kill,
with every hunt and netting,
the more you will lose your way,
the more you will become a wanderer
in the realm of shadows
you used to call "your life."

You will not be physically dead,
but more dead than the dead will you be.
When you no longer can find your way home,
the voices, hands, and embraces of the dead
will hunt and haunt you.

YOUNG ULYSSES: I have learned and participated in such horrors
by sacrificing others.
I have learned that you must navigate your own vessel,
and you must follow your nature and destiny.
This is the lesson of the Promethean fire maker,
even though I have not lived as a fire maker
and fire giver.

BOTH: And let the fires burn.

YOUNG PENELOPE: So that the living can see me.

YOUNG ULYSSES: So that the dead can find me.

YOUNG PENELOPE: To give light to the world,
     you first must burn.

YOUNG ULYSSES: You are one of these women
     who I can neither find nor lose,
     for I am always searching, longing,
     seeking, aching for you.
     You are all women.
     My desire, longing, aching,
     my joy in life.
     I have looked into the veil of mystery
     and I have seen your face.
     I have heard your voice,
     I have touched your breast,
     I have tasted your skin.
     You are the mistress of my body.
     Come to me.

[*PENELOPE embraces him.*]

YOUNG PENELOPE: There is no possible way
     to reach to the bottom of your world.
     There is no possible way to reach
     to the top or the sides.
     You continue swimming. Look!
     And there float your phantoms,
     reaching out for both of us!

     Of all the men I could have been with,
     I chose you,
     not because I am blind to who you are
     and what you have done,

41

but because you have the capacity and humanity
to realise and admit your frailties
and the damage you have caused to others
for your benefit.

I could have been with another,
but I chose you,
for the strength that you have
in your character.

Now ask me,
would I choose another man
before you or after you?
Ask me.

ULYSSES: Would you choose another
before me or after me, Penelope?
And who would you like
for me to bring to you?
Socrates, Plato,
Aristotle, Pericles?
I would surrender you to them
if you so desired.

I want you to have joy
and not be shipwrecked
on the shore of quiet despair
because you are not fully in your life.

So tell me, Penelope,
mistress of my senses and body,
who do you want me to bring to you
to keep your sanity and sexuality burning?

YOUNG PENELOPE: I burn for you!
I do not desire other men.
They are not even sexually desirable to me.
As pleasing as all the men you mentioned

may be to many women,
I can only think of them as my sisters.

YOUNG ULYSSES: Come and kiss me, light of my heart.

[*They hold each other and kiss tenderly.*]

YOUNG PENELOPE: I remember that old philosopher, Socrates,
telling me that if one is to jump
the abyss of separation,
one needs to be a dancer.

YOUNG ULYSSES: Does the abyss separate us?

YOUNG PENELOPE: No, the abyss is all around us.
Imagine if it is all around us,
then we are closer to each other
than we thought.

I sat with him under that old oak tree
for one day and one night
and all the time I wanted to warn him,
to plead with him to become a dancer.

YOUNG ULYSSES: Whatever happened to Socrates?
Did he jump into the abyss?
Did he finally seduce the forest nymphs
or did they seduce him?
Or did they consume him,
or did political man hunt him into the ground?

YOUNG PENELOPE: My poor teacher had to pay with his life
for his dance with the truth of the forest nymphs.

I learned that in order for one
to remain above the ground
one has to have mad dancing feet.
I am a dancer when my nimble feet and toes
dance on the tightrope of my life.

I am found and lost in dance,
"and there is only dance."[27]

YOUNG ULYSSES: Come, my wild forest nymph,
and consume me with your dance.

What do the shepherds
say about wood nymphs?

YOUNG PENELOPE: If you are lucky enough to be sexually consumed
and burned by one,
it is said everyone will know of your ecstasy
for your feet will face backwards.

YOUNG ULYSSES: Come, my wood nymph,
and turn my feet backwards.
Let all the world laugh and say,
"There goes Ulysses!
He has been loved
by Penelope,
for his feet are taking him backwards
rather than forwards."

Is that why you desired our bed
to be carved from a living tree?
We built our bed around this tree.
Did you need to sleep in the embrace of the tree
to feel protected and cherished,
my wood nymph?

YOUNG PENELOPE: You carved birds and the sea
so that when you are not with me,
I can still sleep and wake in our world.
I can still see what you have seen
in your journey into the sea,
into the sky, into the ground,
into the fire of all shaping and forming life.

That tree is alive.
It still breathes and moves
and whispers to me your secrets.

Did you know that in certain parts
there are trees that are
thousands of years old?
And in their deep silence they speak
to the pure heart and devoted soul.

In that carved tree
that we have made our marriage bed
I have given and received,
I have had your seed grow in me.
In that tree I have climbed
and looked into the secrets of the sky.

That tree we sleep on is from my home.
This is our shared world
and the tree will live
as long as we feed it with the seed of our love.

If ever life separates you from me,
no man will come into this room
and no man will sleep under the carvings
that you created from the language of our love.

No man will ever trick me,
making me believe that he is you,
unless he knows the intimacy of our secret.
The key to my bed is the tree.
The planning in my tapestry is the tree.
The beauty of my world is the tree.

YOUNG ULYSSES: *Agape mou,*
my sweet love,
my breath and life,
my blood,

if ever anyone tries to convince you
that they are me,
if ever the world parts us
and you are uncertain,
you can be sure by asking
the man who says he is me,
to describe the carvings.
Ask him about the carvings
that I have engraved to keep your dreams alive.

I have carved the forest,
the trees, the sky
and even the river pebbles for you,
my siren that seeks and finds me
in the deepest seas of my soul.

YOUNG PENELOPE: Ulysses, I can hear horses.
Many horses riding towards our world.
Can you hear them?
An army, a plague is coming our way.

YOUNG ULYSSES: My love, my joy,
let me hold you to me
before they arrive and remove me
from you and our son.

Hold me, for I sense
the hunter and the net are near.
Hold me my love.
You cannot protect me from what is mine,
but I am fox enough to protect you
and our son from what is not theirs.

You belong to no man,
not even me, my wild bird.
Look to your tapestry, your training, your tree
and there you will find me.

[The sound of horses gets louder.
They hold each other and kiss]

YOUNG PENELOPE: It is no other.
   It is your past decisions and actions
   that have arrived to claim you and me,
   to remove you from me.

   It is Agamemnon,

   and the blood you spilled together
   in your past and future wars.

   Shall I lay out the deep red tapestries
   or will I leave this gesture to his wife, Clytemnaestra?
   Such a king should not step on the naked earth,
   for he has soaked it with the blood of men,
   cut down in their prime,
   cut away from their lives,
   cut away from their children.
   Let him walk on the dead bodies
   that have brought him here
   and will take him to Troy.

YOUNG ULYSSES: What have I done?
   What wolves have I killed with,
   and what wolves have I brought to my den?

   Kiss me one more time.
   Hold me close and put your lips to mine.
   Closer, closer.

   Penelope, leave now.
   Leave me now to my past and future decisions
   and the consequences
   that they will have on our lives.

   Hide our son.
   Hide our son

from the darkness of this barbarian,
from this wolf
that would sacrifice his own daughter
to quench his blood thirst
and his excessive appetites.

Leave now!

> [PENELOPE *runs off stage.*
> ULYSSES *closes the door of their secret chamber and the backdrop*
> *indicates a change of scene, into that of a white, barren, cold room.*
> *He awaits Agamemnon's entrance.*]

AGAMEMNON

Colours of Blood

"If we could end the suffering, how we would rejoice.
The spirits brutal hoof has struck our heart
and that is what a woman has to say.
Can you accept the truth?"

(Clytemnaestra)

[The setting is outside the sacred chamber. It is a large, cold room that has a door and a window that faces the courtyard. Agamemnon is a strong, heavyset man, wearing full war armour. He has long, unkempt hair and a beard. His armour has much gold on it. He wears his sword and has some scarring on his face from the wars he has been in. His hair is dark and his eyes darker. He rarely smiles and has an air of arrogance and vanity about him. He is well trained in war, a successful politician, a successful king, a father and husband. He does not look like a monster; he actually looks human, and that is what makes him more dangerous, because one thinks they can negotiate with him and reason with him for the good of others.

ULYSSES stands looking towards the entrance, waiting for AGAMEMNON. AGAMEMNON enters. Stage lighting red.]

ULYSSES: I welcome you into my home, Agamemnon.

AGAMEMNON: My good friend, Ulysses,
    what a glorious day to renew
    our old alliance and friendship.
    We have been through so much
    together, killed so much together,

profited so much together.

We have taken so many adventures together:
you with your clever manoeuvring,
and I with the might and power
of thousands that follow us without question.
Well, if they question we brand them as traitor.
All the glory has been given to me
by others, you and the gods.

I am blessed.

In life you have to take what you want.
It is no good wishing for it
or hoping for it.
You have to take it,
either by persuasion or force.
A real man will never surrender
to obscurity and notoriety.
We both are political animals
and we both know the weakness
of common man,
the need for common man to be told what to do
and when to it.
They can't manage without us,
and therefore they are there for us to use
as we use our horses and cattle and sheep.

Common man is there for us to exploit
and reap the rewards of our conquest of them.

Of course we practice civilised methods.
We have debates and lectures and we pretend to listen
as we portray ourselves as open
to the opinion and welfare of common man,
but to put into practise what they say
would remove us from our privilege and power.

Ulysses, you and I do not know hard labour,
nor do we follow or obey the laws
that confine and bind common man.
Therefore we harvest from their toil and sacrifices,
many things
for our elite way of life
that common man only dreams about.

ULYSSES: Agamemnon, we plan and organise methods
on how to strip the common man, the ordinary man—
the field hand,
the foot soldier,
the servant—
from his human right to live in peace,
to harvest the seeds of his labour,
to watch his family grow,
to stay home
instead of going into wars for you and me.
Profits the collective man will not see.
To die in a foreign shore
with strangers and enemies,
never to see their sons or daughters again.

AGAMEMNON: Oh dear! My friend, you have lost your senses—
this sentimentality for common man.
We make history and therefore the demands
and expectations on us are great.
What a burden I have to carry.
Don't you see the weight upon me,
carrying all these people?
What would they do without me?
But I would gladly carry this burden
for the power and glory that my decisions bring to our nation.

No more talk about this, Ulysses.
I feel particularly good today.
The gods have blessed this mission,

although I had to offer my daughter to them
to appease them.

ULYSSES: So it is true! You have sacrificed your daughter, Iphigenia,
for this war on Troy.

AGAMEMNON: It had to be done.
I have other children.
What would you have me do—
not follow my destiny, Ulysses?

She was such a beautiful girl.

It had to be done, and I did it.
Now that takes courage.

ULYSSES: I am truly sorry.

AGAMEMNON: What are you sorry for?
She wasn't your daughter.
Enough of this!
Let's speak about today.

ULYSSES: Today has not unfolded
and the past is long gone and buried,
as some of our friends
and many of our enemies.

Why have you come to Ithaca?
What business do you have
among the forgotten?
I have changed, Agamemnon.
I am no longer the clever fox
that stole the eggs of future generations.

AGAMEMNON: What is this? Future generations? Eggs?
Have you been in the henhouse too long?
Or have you been under Penelope for too long?

ULYSSES: The spilling of so much blood,
    it has driven me mad.
    I have nightmares
    and am not the man I was.

AGAMEMNON: Too much blood. Too little blood.
    Does it really matter?

ULYSSES: This is the life force of a man
    that we speak about
    and we are pouring it into the ground
    where nothing will grow for it.
    And we do it
    with indifference and contempt.

    Have we been in so many battles
    that we have become indifferent to death?
    Or are we only indifferent
    because it is not our death
    and therefore it does not affect
    our scheme and order of things?

    So I ask you again:
    what business do you have with me?

AGAMEMNON: My good friend,
    you have become philosophical and womanly
    about life and our past together.

    Philosophers and poets and women
    are no good at making decisions about life and death.
    They only talk about things after someone else
    has taken action to improve things.
    They do not have the lust to conquer
    and keep conquering others.

    Philosophers and poets and women lack the might
    to cut away the life from another.

They have a problem with spilling a little human blood.
They are cowards and pathetic in life.

If we all sat around contemplating life
like that poor Socrates,
then I would insist that he drank the hemlock sooner.
Such weakness in the spirit
gives off the stench of apathy and melancholy.

What is the matter with you, Ulysses?

How else are we to take
our civilisation to other worlds?
How are we to educate these barbarians?
How are we meant to bring enlightenment to others?
How are we to liberate people from their oppressors?

Therefore we must go where others fear.
Isn't it our responsibility,
our duty as educated and civilised Greeks,
to take our civilisation to others
who are still barbarians?
The Trojans are barbarians.
I hear King Priam still sleeps with the goats.

ULYSSES: This madness has taken a hold of me, Agamemnon,
and it is this madness that makes me reply as I do.

AGAMEMNON: What madness? This also is a weakness in man.

ULYSSES: I have become slow and cannot think as I used to.
Are you saying that we bring progress and liberation
to a group of people that we invade,
murdering their families
and stealing their land?

AGAMEMNON: What happened to my friend?
What madness has possessed you?
Don't you remember our discussions in the past,

about our duty and responsibility
to civilise and educate so that we can bring our way of life
to these oppressed people?

I want you to come with me, my loyal friend.
You have skills that have proven useful to me in the past
and your skills will prove useful
in the spread of our civilisation to Troy.

We have fought in previous battles
and you have proven yourself clever and shrewd.
I have many men that can fight
and I can use them as fodder in battle.
As soon as they fall I can replace them.
They mean nothing to me.
I do not know them or their mother:
one soldier resembles the other.
They do not question
and they are happy in their ignorance.

Common man does not think.
The ordinary man does not see beyond his backyard.
His nature is cowardly and weak.
That is why he obeys and is told what to do,
told how to think
and told who to kill.

The common man obeys and follows!
Offer them
the gods' approval,
the force of an army,
and the miracle and promise of a better life,
to be sealed with the promise
that the gods will bless them
with an afterlife,
if they die for our cause.

They wear the yoke of service and obedience
like the dumb ox.

They don't think.
They are content to be rewarded with a little food,
little ambition, little houses,
and a little sex.
Could you imagine having a little of anything,
especially a little sex?

What is the matter, Ulysses?
Do you disapprove?
Has wifely sex made you impotent in ambition and war?

I have not known you to be a common man, an ordinary man.
I have seen you disobey and rage, plan,
and murder children in front of their fathers
and women in front of their husbands.
You had a heart of stone.

ULYSSES: I am lost, Agamemnon.
Did I really do those things?
Did my hands murder children and women?

AGAMEMNON: This must be a strange humour
that has fallen upon you.
It must be because you have stayed
with the same woman for too long.

You are vital to me in this war against Troy.
You think, question, and probe,
as you are aware. Your intellect and craft
in manipulating human nature is rare,
and that is why you are my most important advisor.

I do not have clever advisors.
I need your intellectual planning,
your precision in measuring danger

and working with it, to achieve our victory,
at any cost
to our men, to our enemy.
You have always in the past
proven yourself to be clever.
We call you "The Fox" in war.

You know how to read human nature
and outwit all of them.
You plan and organise,
and you know the weakness of the enemy.
You know the weakness in the strongest enemy.
You set traps in persuasion or gifts
and they fall onto your sword,
thinking you are different from me!

That always makes me laugh—
when I see the dying eyes of those you have tricked
into believing your sophistry or accepting your dangerous gifts.
I do enjoy that moment.
It has a triple climax for me:
they realise they are dying
and there is nothing they can do,
they realise they have been betrayed,
and finally, in their dying breath,
they are aware that all their family will also die.

ULYSSES: You fascinate me and disturb me
and you think too much
of my clever ways.
When you and I were in battles together
I was younger and did not measure danger.
Instead I took it on,
and by chance and luck
I managed to remain alive,
and by manipulation and cunning
I managed to slaughter many.

By chance and luck
the enemy made the mistake of believing me.
It wasn't because I can read human nature;
it was chance and luck.
Fear makes men believe in the devil.
If they believe they will be spared;
there was no great strategy there—
only deception.

AGAMEMNON: You have grown humble in your old age, my old friend.

ULYSSES: Winning a war or losing it
depends on arriving in the night,
pretending to be someone you are not,
gaining their confidence,
infiltrating and causing conflict within the community,
and attacking a country that does not have
the military might we have.
And if we can't do it that way?
We will offer them gifts
and in the night we will murder all that sleep,
thinking that the danger has passed.

AGAMEMNON: I have won all my wars.

ULYSSES: We have always won
because we are always planning wars.
Even in peace we are planning against our neighbours.

We lived all the diplomatic displays of peace
while we planned legally,
ways to net and occupy the lands of others.
This takes a certain type of methodical
and organised cleverness,
a certain corruptive banal evil.
It doesn't look evil, but it is,
for it destroys the lives of many
for the profit of a few.

We managed to catch the enemy sleeping,
unguarded and unprotected,
and his women and children sleeping—
so warm, so fresh, so sweet.
They never woke up
with our swords piercing their hearts,
and in that sleep
they must have thought
they were having a nightmare,
with death,
a nightmare they never woke up from.

AGAMEMNON: I remember how I cut them from their lives,
both women and children as they slept.
We murdered all the "pretty ones."[28]

ULYSSES: War is about killing.
How smart do you have to be to kill?

AGAMEMNON: You don't have to be smart to kill,
but you do have to be smart
to get a whole country to follow your orders to kill,
to kill men that they have not met,
men who have never harmed them,
men just like them, with children and families.

Now you will have to agree
that getting a whole country to kill for you
is a task that requires a man
who has surpassed the needs and appetites of the ordinary man.
It takes a certain type of will
that is not in sympathy with humanity,
a certain type of heart that needs to be stone,
and a certain type of courage
shown in willingness to kill his own daughter
to achieve more lands for his country.

I am such a man.
I have no remorse or regret.
I am of the strongest of men,
the most noble and the most respected of men.
We are the protectors of civilisation and democracy.

ULYSSES: We civilised men
depend on the fear of others.
We implant fear in our own and in our enemy.
They respect and obey us out of fear:
the fear of what we might do to them if they do not obey,
the fear of what we might do their wives and children.
Their respect and obedience is based in fear.

We have the military might.
We have the persuasive arguments and rhetoric.
We have the winner's history.
We have no opposing voices.

AGAMEMNON: Why, if we did not have men such as these,
we would be overrun by the hordes
of uncivilised barbarians
destroying the order and balance
that we have had handed down
from our forefathers.

The order and balance
that we have worked too hard to maintain.

I want you to accompany me and my army to Troy.
My brother's wife, Helen, has been abducted
from her home and taken by Paris to Troy.
My brother's heart is broken by the loss
of his most loved and faithful wife.

Helen was taken without her consent.
A free woman, a faithful and loving wife
was taken by force.

What type of man would I be
if I did not want to storm Troy
and release her from this barbaric captivity?

Today it is Helen;
tomorrow it may be our wives that these barbarians
can come, rape, and abduct from us.

ULYSSES: And you will storm Troy! What have you done to prevent this bloodshed?

AGAMEMNON: How could we ever be called free men,
defenders of reason and democracy,
if we cannot bring freedom
to the oppressed and imprisoned?
What type of men are we if we cannot free one of our women?

And since you already speak as a wise man,
a philosopher, then you clearly understand
that I have no other choice.
I have tried political negotiating with them,
but it has not worked. They are barbarians.
The Trojans have left me with no other choice
than to go and bring Helen back
to her husband and people.

I have sent messages to King Priam
asking for the release of Helen
but the messengers have not returned.
It is obvious that these poor wretches
have been killed for taking a message
of Reason and Concern
to the barbarian king.

We have no other choice.
We are going to Troy to bring back Helen.
Think how terrible it would be for her,
for she is a woman of virtue and faithfulness

to her husband, my brother.

Think how vile her life must be
among those barbarians
that look upon her as their whore,
and Paris, who forced and forces himself upon her.
It is too violent to think about.

Woman is meant to be protected,
not brutalised and dehumanised
through submission and rape.
We are civilised men.
Women are important in my life and kingdom.
They all have a purpose,
and I will not allow such a brutal crime
as to steal one of our women.

What type of men would we be
if we allowed others to steal
what belongs to us?

What type of message would we
be sending to others?

ULYSSES: My messengers have told me
that Helen fell in love with Paris,
for they say that he is young and handsome,
has a young and strong body
and is a Prince in his own right,
with influence and knowledge.
They say he is educated.
If that is the case, there is no kidnapping
or a victim to be rescued,
is there?

AGAMEMNON: My poor brother Menelaus is heartbroken.
He cannot eat or drink.
He wants his faithful and beloved wife back.

It is important to get Helen back
for he has become a laughing stock.
Among our men, he is known as "a cuckold."
It is important to our honour
that we be given the satisfaction
of revenge and retribution for this crime.

ULYSSES: Since when has it been a crime to love?

Since when has it been criminal
for a wife to fall out of love
with her older husband
and lust for a younger and wealthier man?
Helen lusted for Paris's body and wealth
and from what I hear,
he could have had any woman in either kingdom,
without abducting or forcing himself upon her.

Let me get this right:
Are you saying to me that this war on Troy
is a war for justice and the liberation of Helen?
Are you saying that this war must happen
so that we can correct this evil?
Are you saying that Paris has brought
destruction to your home
and that so many thousands of men
on both sides need to be involved in this war
so that you and your brother do not lose your honour?

But that is not the truth, is it?

That is the emotional lie that you have given
as truth to the ordinary man,
the emotional truth that an enemy has taken one
of our women, and therefore no woman is safe.
The emotional truth that we as "civilised" men
must and need to bring justice to this injustice.

Or is the truth that Troy is a wonderful and rich land
to conquer?

Or do we need to conquer
so that we burn the truth?
And in these fires from hell
we will sacrifice many, many men
from both our army and the army of Troy.

AGAMEMNON: I thought I could appeal
to your sense of liberating a victim,
liberating one of our women,
to your sense of honour and duty
as an educated and civilised man.

I do not need to defend myself.
I do not need to explain myself to you.
It is my family and country
that has been violated.
I do not need to give you or any man
explanations, reasons, or excuses,
for I have might on my side.
And with might
I can shape, transform, or alter the truth.

ULYSSES: You have not changed, Agamemnon.
You have twisted and turned the facts
to fit your ambitions and agenda,
to accumulate more lands.
You have corrupted the truth
and turned night into day
and day into night
by telling others
that this war is to liberate,
this war is to stop this injustice,
this war we must have.

AGAMEMNON: I have the honour of my house and country
    to uphold. This war
    will make things right again.
    will bring justice and retribution
    to the innocent and the guilty.

    These Trojan barbarians will never again
    bring harm or threat to the world of civilised man.

    I will not wait for this crime
    to dissolve or to be forgotten.
    I will not forgive or forget.
    Troy will burn!
    I will not wait for Paris to come with his armies
    and take my home and country from me.
    I believe we are in danger
    of invasion from these barbarians,
    and our world of reason and civilisation
    will flicker and die out, if we do not act,
    if we do not invade them before they invade us.

    The element of surprise will work for us:
    we will net and kill them while they sleep.
    We must protect our people and our world,
    and therefore I will need all my good advisors
    to assist me with this invasion.

ULYSSES: You do know what you are doing.
    How could you not know?
    For you have planned and convinced
    the army and the population
    that this war that we must have
    is for a noble reason,
    for justice,
    for the fear of being invaded by Troy,
    and for the promotion and spread of civilisation.

You have convinced the army
that this war is noble and is blessed by the gods.
I mean, look at you, you love your country so much
that no sacrifice is too small or too great for you:
to even put your blade through your daughter's heart
to justify your actions to your gods,
to convince the army,
to make them believe in your greatness
and love for your country.
That you would even sacrifice
your own daughter for this cause!
The *cause* of justice and the spread of our civilisation!

This war is not about Helen.
She is no one of importance to you, or your brother.
She may have hurt your brother's vanity
by leaving with a beautiful young man,
but this war is not about Helen.
She is only the scapegoat for something bigger,
sinister and darker.
You are not going to war
for our country and the spread of our civilisation,
You are going to war for the pillage of Troy
and her riches.
This is about genocide,
for no one will live in Troy again
once we start the fires of war.

You never disappoint me, Agamemnon.
Just when I thought you could go no further into the abyss,
you come back from the deepest darkness
with the teeth and nails of all the creatures from that darkness.

AGAMEMNON: Thank you for your admiration, Ulysses.
I also have learned much from you
but you do not disappoint me.
You do understand the thoughts behind my actions.

You do understand the ways of men like me.
You understand them because you are of them.

You are not this meek and melancholy philosopher or poet
but rather a shrewd and cunning man
who has advised me on many night slaughters.

Now listen and understand me.
I will allow you to speak your thoughts
in the privacy of this room,
just to show to you what a democratic
and compassionate man I am
towards you.

This will be the only time
you will voice your thoughts
and when you have finished
telling me what you have practised
in manipulation, agendas and going to war,
you will accompany me to Troy.

ULYSSES: I am not able to do that, Agamemnon.
I am not your fox or bloodhound.
My thoughts are scattered and lost.
Listen to the way I have spoken to you.
In the past I was the one planning all this,
and now I am lost in my mind.
I seem to have lost my senses,
lost my abilities to navigate in life and war.
I would be useless and a weight to you.

AGAMEMNON: I suggest you remember your place, Ulysses,
and I suggest you remember my power
and do not make me forget
that we have been united in brotherhood
through the blood of many,
for I value you as my advisor.

ULYSSES: Agamemnon, you weave the truth
and the lie in the same thread.
Then you twist and wrap it
around the throat of the unsuspecting,
like an unwanted umbilical cord.
And you pull and pull
until you get submission or death.

In my madness
I can see Iphigenia's death,
the death of your daughter.
Is it true that her last words to you were
"Father, have you no heart?"

"Did you not wrap her around and around
in her gowns so that she could not move?
Did you not seal her mouth
so that we would not hear her pleas and curses?"[29]

I am sure we would have heard her pleas in Ithaca.
We would have heard her
had you not sealed her mouth
and then proceeded to seal her eyes and her life.

AGAMEMNON: This is the law, and the law is the law.
I am bound by the laws of my country.

This has been a yoke of necessity—
to have no personal life
because my people, my country
come before my needs as a man.

Do not moralise to me!

How many men can sacrifice their own child
to prove their love for their country?
Can you? I suspect you could.
You did not spare other men's children in war.

ULYSSES: There is also another law,
    and that is "blood will have blood."[30]

AGAMEMNON: There you go again, moralising to me.
    Is this the madness you are suffering from?
    Iphigenia, my poor daughter.
    If only she knew how much
    she has blessed with her blood
    this war of honour and justice.

    I ask you once again
    to remember your place and position,
    for I will not suffer this weakness in you.
    I will not suffer your moralising to me.

    I love and loved my daughter.
    This was the most painful duty I had to conduct.
    I had to offer part of me as an offering
    so that the army could see that I was and am
    a man of honour and self-sacrifice.
    I am so bound in the laws of our land,
    the laws of our gods,
    the laws of our civilised code and way of life,
    that I would and could
    cut into the heart of my daughter.

    Is there any greater loss to a father
    than to offer his child as a sacrifice
    to save his country?

    It was difficult but achievable.
    Could you have done it?
    With those bloodstained hands,
    could you have done it?

    Don't judge me as an ordinary man,
    for I am of the land of the law,
    of the blood of the land,

and of the people.

My will is of metal and my heart is of stone.
How do you think I have become master over so many lives?
By showing weakness in emotion?
Practising humanitarian acts of kindness and justice
to those I need to use and harvest
to bring expansion and glory for my country?

Your country, Ulysses.

You should be praising me.
It does not matter what you have to do
as long as gain and profit is the result.

And well you know that the ordinary man
does not want to think and make decisions.
He is cowardly and lazy, and that is why
I have the power and permission from my people
to keep them in the privileges they are used to.
They do not want to lose their way of life and living,
and therefore we need to continue
our expansion and conquest of others.

ULYSSES: Great, Agamemnon.
What a great political animal you are.
And when you stop the rhetoric,
it comes down to the ground
where the blood has been spilled,
where it will continue to be spilled.

You and I are murderers of the young and innocent.

AGAMEMNON: A murderer, Ulysses?
How do you think you became master of all these lands?
Did you not murder men, women, and children in their sleep?
So that you can become a master in this land.
So that you can have servants doing your work in the fields.

So that you can fornicate all day and night without worrying
about earning your living by working.
How do you think you got this privileged life?
How do you think you got these lands
and these rights that other men do not have?

Do you still insist that you are mad?

ULYSSES: You are right. I have done all these things.
    I am lost.
    I am confused.
    I am losing my mind.

AGAMEMNON: So be it! Enough!
    [*To a soldier outside the door*] Take Ulysses son.
    He must be outside. I saw him as I came in.
    Bring two strong horses and tie
    one on the left arm of his son
    and the other on the right arm,
    and then ask the soldier to get the horses to run
    in different directions.
    Do this now!

    Come, Ulysses, to the window,
    so that you can see.
    Since you are claiming that you are mad,
    you will neither know the danger nor care.

[*Screams are heard from Telemachus, Ulysses's son.*]

TELEMACHUS [*offstage*]: [*screaming*] Father, where are they taking me?

AGAMEMNON: Come, Ulysses.
    This cutting in half of your son
    will feed and keep your madness.

[*PENELOPE enters the room to ask what is happening.*]

AGAMEMNON: Good of you to join us, Penelope.
    Obviously you are looking for your screaming son.
    He's out in the courtyard with my men.

[*PENELOPE moves towards the door.*]

AGAMEMNON: Stop. If you leave this room, that boy is dead
    before you get to the courtyard.

[*PENELOPE draws closer to ULYSSES.*]

    Come, Penelope.
    Come and watch the cutting in half of your son.
    I think the black horse will do more damage.
    It seems stronger than the grey one.
    I like children.
    Actually, I love children.
    I recently lost one of my pretty ones
    and feel closer to her
    by watching the cutting in half of yours.

    Tell me, Penelope,
    is it true that your husband has tried to trick me
    by pretending that he is mad?
    Why, only a mad man would put salt in his fields,
    and only a mad man will allow
    his son to be torn limb from limb as he watches.

    The lengths to which men go
    to stay in a woman's bed.

    Is he mad, Penelope?
    Can you confirm or deny
    either his sanity or his clever insanity?

ULYSSES: [*having been frozen to the window that overlooks the court yard*]
    Stop! Tell them to untie my son and bring him back to his mother!

[*AGAMEMNON looks out the window into the courtyard and orders his men to stop.*]

AGAMEMNON: Untie the boy, but leave him with you, until I finish
    speaking with Ulysses.

ULYSSES: Leave my son and wife out of this matter.
    This is between you and me.

AGAMEMNON: What is this I hear?
    You are not mad, Ulysses?
    You have tried to trick me?
    Shame on you, Ulysses,
    for now you have made angry.
    And you know what a damaging emotion this is for me.
    Speak to me, Ulysses.

ULYSSES: Do not involve my son or wife in this.

AGAMEMNON: You have involved them by hiding the truth from me.
    So how can I not involve them
    when you have refused to come with me because of them?
    You leave me no choice.

    Penelope, has your husband grown old
    and slow in his wits?
    In the old days
    he would have jumped at the chance
    to bring honour and fame to his country.
    He would have invented the war
    to gain more land and wealth.
    Now he complicates the life of his family
    and this war with a madness that he claims he has,
    and worse—this madness stinks
    of manipulation and deception!
    Shame on you, Ulysses, for trying to trick me
    with your martial cleverness.

I think he has become this way
because he has not been in battle.
He has lost the purpose and direction of what a man must do.
Rather he has been sitting here in Ithaca and rotting,
devising a clever insanity
so that I can declare him mad
and leave him here to rut and fornicate.

PENELOPE: Please spare my son's life.
My husband makes his own decisions
with or without my approval.
Let me go and get my son and give him lunch.

AGAMEMNON: Leave him there with my men for a little while longer.
Some of my men love young boys,
and they have not seen one in some time.

Penelope, my messengers tell me
of your wit, your humour,
your discipline, and your prowess with the sword.
You are an accomplished woman.
You have rights and your own ideas—
although, at this very moment
you look dumb and stupid,
helpless and anxious for the safety of your son.

Come, Penelope,
Defend or betray your husband.
It makes no difference to me.
So much for your wit.
Look at you, standing there, like a mute.
One can be witty when she is comfortable
and with friends.
Now that you have a crisis, Penelope,
you are tongueless.
I can arrange that also!

ULYSSES: Agamemnon, let me appeal to you,
    for all the things that we have done together,
    for all the times that we have saved each other's lives.

AGAMEMNON: Stop, Ulysses. I am having fun.
    Tell me, Penelope,
    is your old husband losing his senses?
    Is he going to be useless to me in Troy?
    Will he serve you better to stay in your bed?
    Let me hear your voice and wit, Penelope.

PENELOPE: There are stages for all things
    and phases in life.
    Ulysses is older and is forgetful and neglectful
    in simple and complex things
    concerning the running of Ithaca.
    Therefore, he should be admired
    for seeking to serve you
    with sincerity and a moral conscience
    by telling you of his weakness.

AGAMEMNON: I am surrounded by well-rehearsed actors.
    So what you are telling me is that your husband,
    a man that has made blood vows to me,
    is really mildly mad
    and that he has a moral fibre
    for speaking the truth to me?
    So you are going to protect your husband's bad judgement
    and make him out to be an ethical man?
    Ulysses, an *ethical* man?

    Did I miss anything?

ULYSSES: Allow my wife and son to leave so that we can speak as men.

AGAMEMNON: Now this is deep for me, Ulysses.
    I don't remember being anything else but a man.
    Sentimentality is wasted on me, Ulysses.

Now let me tell you what I am going to do.
I will tear your son limb from limb with those horses outside,
and you will have two of him.
Or will I give him to my men
as I have told you before.
There are men in my army that are especially fond of young boys.

ULYSSES: Stop, Agamemnon! Stop!

AGAMEMNON: No, Ulysses.
You have taken me this far
and now I will take you further than you want to go.
I will take you and your family into brutality and hell.

ULYSSES: I have served you and have assisted you
in your accumulation of wealth and power.
I have been stained by the same enemies' blood.
I have fought side by side with you.
We have saved each other's lives in many war struggles.

AGAMEMNON: I have told you before that I can go further into hell.
I think you stop at the gate.
I come from there and live there,
and will bring this hell to your wife and son.
I will finish what you cannot.
You should have not started this clever madness with me.
You should not have tested my patience and
blood vows that I have taken with you in the past.
You will stand quietly while I tell you
what I will do with your wife,
the one that you want to stay with.
You will not interrupt me again
while I take you into this the great suffering
that involves your son's and wife's destiny at my hands,
at my men's hands.

I will consume her physically—and you know I am carnivorous—
burn your lands,

kill your servants and villagers.
My men can get some practice on your kindred:
they are a little restless.

I will not kill you.
I will make you watch.
I will have you tied to the bed.

After I have violently consumed your wife
and she has surrendered to me,
I will hand what is left of her to my men
who have not seen a woman for some time.
And the last man who has her
will decide what her fate will be.
Maybe she will be returned to me—
but I do not feed on the meat
that other men have fornicated on and have eaten from. [*He goes over to Penelope and puts his hand on her groin.*]

PENELOPE: I would rather die!

AGAMEMNON: But you will!
But not before giving pleasure to me and to many other men.
And you, Ulysses, will be tied to the bed.
You will watch it all!
And after we have finished
and burned everything,
you will come with me to Troy,
and you will advise me on matters of war.

ULYSSES: Why would I come with you after you have killed everyone I love?

AGAMEMNON: Thank you, Ulysses.
See how intelligent your wits are?
You are right.
Why would you come
if you have nothing to live for?

So I'll tell you what I will do instead.

We will take Penelope with us to Troy and we will all share her.
We will also take your son,
so the men in my army who are fond of young boys
can share him.
That way they are alive and you will be useful to me.

Does this please you more?

ULYSSES: I will come with you and I will serve you as I did before.
Let my wife and son go, I beg you.

AGAMEMNON: It is not enough that you just come with me.
I want you to be involved in this war with a full heart.
That is the only way you will be useful
to me and my men.
If you do not come of your own free will,
I will keep your wife and son alive
but they will be sexual servants to me and my men.

Sometimes, my friend,
there are worse things than death.

ULYSSES: I will come on my own free will and with a full heart.

AGAMEMNON: [looks out the window and yells to his men] Let the boy go.
Go to your son, Penelope.
Your husband has seen reason
and has been healed from his madness.
The gods have given me such powers.

ULYSSES: I will come.
I will come of my free will and a full heart.
I pledge myself to this cause and this war.
I will not speak the truth to our men.

We will destroy Troy,
their language and culture.

We will make their world in our image
and everyone will have our culture by force,
our way of life.

I am happy to open the doors to hell
and Agamemnon. And I will follow
and cut down the generations of my enemy,
who have the distorted reason of hate,
the desire to obliterate other men's lives
as if they are a plague of locusts.

Or are we the plague?

I will come with you
and I will assist you in this quest.

AGAMEMNON: Good thinking, Ulysses.
Nothing like a crisis to bring you back to us.

My dear Ulysses, not being in battle
has left you with a twisted depth.
I have come at the right time.
This journey will lift your spirits
and fill your coffers.

I have come at the right time.
Had I left you any longer in Ithaca
you would have followed in the footsteps of Socrates.
I mean, what was his use in life?
Death has improved him, don't you think?

We can't have philosophers,
poets, or anarchists
running reason and civilisation.

I have seen many men die.
I have slaughtered many men.
I have no regrets.
I have slaughtered my own daughter.

And you must coil and coil
the thread of life around and around
the throat of the unsuspecting,
and then you pull them down
and strike hard into their heart.
All the while they will feel
surprise, fear, or even betrayal.

You see, Ulysses, you could not sacrifice you son.
Therefore, I am a stronger, nobler man.

Men surrender quicker
when you betray them
with the threat of slaughtering their "pretty ones"[31]
and sexually consuming their wives.

It always works. And that is why, my Ulysses,
you must never love—
wives, children, men
are there for you to use as tools,
to gain power, fame, prestige, wealth.
This is who we are and this is how we have what we have.
We certainly have not worked for it.
Have *you*?

ULYSSES: We certainly have not worked for it,
    like the ox
    and like the peasants in the field.

AGAMEMNON: This is how you become a collector of many men!
    You break them in spirit
    and you collect them
    in the hunt of the night.
    Coil around and around their throats
    the thread of distortion and deception
    and then strike!
    Deep,
    deep,

deeper.
Until nothing remains pulsing,
flowing, beating, moving.

We have hunting to do, Ulysses.
Bring your nets.
We have many wild creatures to catch
in the sky, in the sea
and on the soil of Troy.

Come, Ulysses, you clever fox.
Take me to the eggs of their next generations
so that I can smash all of them.

[*ULYSSES and AGAMEMNON exit. YOUNG PENELOPE and PENELOPE start the chorus. The tapestry is war scenes and the colour is deep red.*]

YOUNG PENELOPE: Dear God, set me free from all the pain.
    "And when I keep to my bed, soaked in dew,
    And the thoughts go groping through the night,
    And the good dreams that used to guard my sleep.

    Not here.
    Terror, is at my neck."[32]

PENELOPE: "And swooping lower, all could see,
    plunging their claws into a hare, a mother
    bursting with unborn young—the babies spilling
    quick spurts of blood—cut off! the race just dashing into life!
    Blood will have blood.

BOTH: Blood will have blood
    and suffer, suffer into truth."[33]

YOUNG PENELOPE: "They are kneeling by the bodies of the dead,
    embracing men and brothers,
    infants over the aged loins that gave them life, and sobbing,
    as the yoke constricts their last free breath,
    for every dear one lost."[34]

PENELOPE: And what of Agamemnon's men?
  Ashes and urns come back.

BOTH: "Blood will have blood.
  A man's lifeblood
  is dark and mortal
  once it wets the earth.
  What song can sing it back?"[35]

YOUNG PENELOPE: War is a creature
  that has the legs of many men,
  the heads of a few,
  and the arms of millions
  that will tear man, woman, and child into pieces.

PENELOPE: War is a living creature
  that feeds on human blood.
  It grows in its blind rage, seeking for more human blood.
  It is organised by a select few:
  the keepers of culture,
  the keepers of intellectual power and knowledge,
  the keepers of the secrets of the beast.

BOTH: It is kept alive by many.

PENELOPE: They feed it human flesh and human blood:
  the flesh and blood of both
  the kindred and the stranger.
  The creature of war has no voice
  because its mouth is full with human flesh;
  therefore, its makers and keepers
  will speak in a peaceful voice
  "designed to make lies sound truthful
  and murder respectable."[36]

YOUNG PENELOPE: This creature called war
  grows from all its devouring,
  from all the loss and grief of others.

It mutates the truth within the rotting corpses
into a mass rage and grief without relief—
a blind rage and deep grief
that words can never give relief.

PENELOPE: Some doors are not meant to be opened,
and all who pass those doors
"abandon all hope."[37]

BOTH: Once we have lost
the anchor and the thread to our life
it is the animals that pity man.

[*Note: The Chorus has been interwoven with sections from the Chorus from Aeschylus's* The Oresteia *and Euripides's thoughts on war,* The Trojan Women.

This section is not intended to glorify war or to shock the reader; it is there to engender thought and compassion for those caught up in wars or who have come from wars. If enough of us realise the price of war on both sides, we might, as evolved people, consider not making war on our neighbours and realise that we all need to live on this planet, and we all need to share its resources in peace and humanity. I have put this section in to expose some of the horrors of war and to cause reflection, connection, compassion, and a more evolved way of addressing our problems, as a humane world community.]

ACT IV
UNDER HOUSE ARREST

Colours of the Sea

[*The PENELOPE that we meet in this dialogue and scene is more controlled and planning. She is standing by the shoreline, looking into the sea, reflecting on her thoughts.*]

PENELOPE: The nets of the wolf and the jackal
    have been thrown over Ithaca.
    The hunters, the opportunists, the thieves
    and the murderers live just outside my door.
    I am under house arrest.

    Right across from my courtyard
    they have come, presenting themselves
    as cultivated men,
    as educated men,
    as civilised men.

    While all the while I can see their plans and nets,
    their claws and smiling white teeth,
    the teeth of the jackal and wolf
    before they tear into the soft flesh of their prey.
    They wait for the bait to fall
    into their foaming mouth.
    Are these men, wild dogs, or wolves?
    I watch them from my courtyard.
    They all have become a family that works together
    in secrecy and crime
    for the prize: the fall of Ithaca,
    the bedding and betrayal of me,
    the murder of my son.

[*AGATHY: About thirty-five. He is handsome and lusts for PENELOPE and her lands. He is a brute. AGATHY has a solid build, the body of a warrior, with dark long hair and dark eyes. He has no scarring on his body, as he has not gone to war, having led a privileged and protected existence. His hands are thick and heavy, like his intellect, and all culture and the fine arts are wasted on him. He is vain, proud, and arrogant and cannot detect when he is being mocked. He truly believes that Zeus gave him birth.*

PETROCULOS: About fifty-five. Intellectual, patient, experienced in political and personal life, he wants to achieve domination, not only of Ithaca but the whole region. He accomplishes things through persuasion and gets others to do the physical violence when required. PETROCULOS is a tall, lean, elderly man with the look of education. He too has not gone to war but has given advice on many. His hair and beard are grey; he gives the impression of being your kind grandfather and "sister," and therefore others trust him easily.

PETROCULOS and AGATHY are speaking together discussing an alliance to work together so that they can outwit the other suitors and PENELOPE. If AGATHY shows aggression towards PENELOPE, she will ask assistance from PETROCULOS, sealing the deal between them: they both will share in the region's wealth.]

PETROCULOS: Look my boy,
    you will have to overcome
    your sexual impulses towards Penelope,
    because if the other suitors find out
    that we have hurt her in any way
    or that we are working together
    in terrorizing and befriending her,
    they will kill both of us.

AGATHY: I understand.
    We can't seem to have an advantage
    or spoil the balance of terror that is in place.

PETROCULOS: Penelope is to never suspect or know
    of our conspiracy against her.
    She must believe that she chose one of us

of her own free will.

All are here to make sure
that Penelope chooses one of them
and everyone here believes it will be he.

To disturb this "balance"
would cause chaos and murder among us,
and the strongest,
or the one who is not murdered in his sleep
will be left standing, and probably not for long.

Another factor that you have forgotten
is that your future wife, Penelope,
is also trained and disciplined
with the sword and rhetoric.
Therefore such a situation of disturbance
would give her the advantage.

AGATHY: You are saying that Penelope and her son,
The Doubtful as he is known,
would seize this opportunity
to organise and fight or manage to flee,
that some from the other islands
may come to assist her.

PETROCULOS: She is admired and wanted
by the men who have been here for ten years.
If they did not admire and lust for her
then at any time they could have
stormed and taken over her little Ithaca.

I tell you this woman has charm, wit, and seduction,
and let's not forget she is as cunning and as clever as her Ulysses.

AGATHY: Yes! Yes! We must keep it in the law
or at least make it look as if we have not broken the law—
or not get caught when we are breaking it.

PETROCULOS: We must keep it planned, organised,
    civilised and conduct ourselves as men with honour.

AGATHY: How do we conduct ourselves by night?

PETROCULOS: The night has not eyes,
    and you can conduct yourself as you please,
    as long as you do not get caught.
    As civilised and cultured men,
    we must convince all others, including Penelope,
    that it is she who will make the decision.

AGATHY: Woman, making her own decision,
    with her own free will!
    I tell you, it is not healthy for her sexually.
    My father told me to allow a woman
    such freedom would affect her bodily fluids
    and that she would become dry and frigid.

PETROCULOS: We must make all others believe
    that we are following
    the law of the land and our ancestors.
    It is called politics, rhetoric.
    Our civilisation is based on such lies and trickery.
    You never reveal the real agenda
    until you have the transaction of expansion and possession
    sealed, netted, and bled.

AGATHY: I don't bother myself
    with such complicated political explanations.
    My main drive is here [*puts his hand on his genital area*]
    and I don't need a sexual lecture
    or political training from you, old man;
    I know how to conduct myself with a woman.
    I know what they want.

    When they say no they mean yes.
    It's their way of being difficult,

to make a man wild with passion.

PETROCULOS: Who gave you this pearl of wisdom?

AGATHY: My father and my grandfather,
    and I have watched the sheep and goats.
    Women are similar. You have to overpower them
    to make them feel wanted.
    Women call this foreplay.
    I see a woman, I tell her she is beautiful
    like no other
    and she believes me and is happy.

    She says no,
    I say yes,
    she says no,
    I say yes.

    But eventually,
    after a few minutes of such physical struggle,
    she will please me sexually.
    God, it has been a long time
    since I have been with a young woman.
    All the women on this accursed island
    are as old as my grandfather,
    and some of them look just like him.

PETROCULOS: Poor boy. Are you telling me
    that Penelope's handmaidens and servants
    are not to your liking—or lusting?
    Or are you telling me your charm
    does not work with any of them?

    AGATHY: You don't have sexual needs like I do.
    You are old and dried up.
    I have been here for ten long years.
    I came here when I was twenty-five,
    on this accursed rock they call Ithaca,

and that woman in there
has refused me her bed.

I don't think she is normal.
I am at the peak of my youth and sexuality,
and she refuses me as her husband.

PETROCULOS: Has anyone on this wretched island,
sunbaking in her courtyard,
been in her chambers?

AGATHY: I have tried to bribe one of her maids
to just let me see Penelope's bedroom,
and all I got was
"There is something living in the mistress's bedroom.
It is something that Ulysses left for her, and it is living."

PETROCULOS: What do you think that is?

AGATHY: A wild animal that she keeps chained
to the bed or in the room?
How could she go without sex for so long?
I tell you she is not normal.

Any other woman would have been
running into my arms
begging me to have sex with her.
And it would have been I,
taking my time, setting the conditions
and convincing her that marrying me
was the best decision she had ever made
in her entire life.

PETROCULOS: Ulysses is dead.
The sea has consumed him
and spat him out as a dead fish on the shore.

AGATHY: I have more than what he had [*again he touches his genitals*].
I have youth and beauty

and a mighty healthy respect and appreciation of woman.

PETROCULOS: Has that tapestry not finished yet?
    You can't go near her room to find out.

AGATHY: You can't go near her!
    Have you ever tried walking beside her on one of her walks?
    You can feel her concealed knife
    that she keeps on her upper arm
    rubbing against your ribs if you dare get near her.
    As soon as that wretched tapestry is finished,
    as soon as that useless material with threads is finished,
    she will choose me,
    and she will be lucky to have me
    in her cold and empty womb.

PETROCULOS: Ah, the fire of youth!
    So you are telling me what I already know.
    Penelope does not find you an Adonis.
    I cannot see why not!

    She can probably hear your knuckles
    scraping the ground as you approach her.
    Let me amend that:
    not only your knuckles but your full testicles also.

AGATHY: I thank you for telling me what is obvious—
    that I possess male potency.
    It has to do with your male glands,
    and this gives off a certain odour
    that women—any woman—finds irresistible.
    I am a real man.

PETROCULOS: And is your aroma a seasonal thing?
    Or do you have the good fortune
    to have this sexual smell about you all the year?

AGATHY: Penelope lusts for me.
She just doesn't want to have a war on her hands
among the suitors,
and she is following the law.
I am not like those others
who lie about in her courtyard
waiting to catch a glimpse of her
or to speak with her on her walks.

PETROCULOS: I heard one reading poetry to her,
another philosophy,
another comforting her about Ulysses's absence.

AGATHY: I mean, what does all that courting prove?
Nothing. Not a thing.
It is all about sex.
And why wait for later
when you can have it yesterday or now?

My father told me the worst thing
you can do with a woman
is to give her too much freedom.
Well, that is how he explained it
when my mother ran away from him
with another woman!

PETROCULOS: And how did your father
explain the loss of your mother to another woman?

AGATHY: It was obvious
my mother could not find another like him
and she would remain faithful to him all her life.
That is why she chose a woman for companionship.

PETROCULOS: Have you not heard of Sappho from Lesbos?

AGATHY: I have heard of Lesbos the island,
but what is a Sappho?

Is it some type of food they eat there?

PETROCULOS: Agathy, Agathy, my boy.
    Look upon me as your father
    or at least your older brother
    and take my advice concerning Penelope.

    You are correct in observing
    that she is not your *ordinary*, mediocre woman.
    She has had philosophers and poets as teachers,
    and Ulysses as her lover and advisor
    who has encouraged her vibrant
    and charismatic temperament.

    She is respected by others in the region
    for her patience, intelligence and wisdom
    in the affairs of her home and country.
    If that is not enough,
    she is as accomplished in battle as you are.

AGATHY: Are you telling me
    that I would have to swordfight with her
    before she took me to bed?
    What a woman!
    She really knows how to consume, drain, and exhaust.

    PETROCULOS: You would not be saying
    that if you had her sharp blade pressing up your throat,
    or better still—up your left testicle!
    And as for her not having sex—
    is she ever without Ulysses?
    When I have spoken with her
    I can see both of them swimming
    in the sea of her eyes.

    You will need more than what you know,
    more and maybe less
    than what your father has taught you about woman.

And do not watch the sheep or goats anymore!
They are seasonal, bad-tempered, and have a bad smell.

AGATHY: So what do you want me to do?
How does one seduce Penelope?

PETROCULOS: I don't think you can seduce her.
I don't think any man will ever seduce her.
She is like the stars in the sky.
You can look upon them
but you cannot change their direction.

And since we follow the stars
to find our way to the shore
and our way home
we also must follow Penelope
to find her weakness in the law,
her bed, her wealth and kingdom.

She has the ability to see into appearances
and is not fooled by flattery.

Her weakness is her son.
He is inexperienced in life and in battle
and reads poetry.
He depends on Penelope.

Her strength is Ulysses.
He is always with her even in his absence.
There is something living
and connecting between them—even in absence.

What we need to do
is to make sure she chooses me for her husband
when the time comes,
when this wretched tapestry is finished.

I have seen through her craftiness and cunning ways.
She is using the tapestry to gain time,

hoping that Ulysses will return in time.

AGATHY: He will not come back.
　　　He is dead or swimming with the sirens.
　　　And even if he does come back
　　　I will make sure he is murdered
　　　before he reaches Penelope.

　　　Penelope *will* have to choose.
　　　By being clever she has used the laws of the land
　　　to protect her.
　　　But now the laws of the land
　　　will coil and coil around her pretty neck
　　　and pull her into my bed.
　　　[*Beat*]
　　　And what do you mean—choose you?

PETROCULOS: Penelope must be forced, through fear
　　　to choose me.
　　　The other suitors out in the courtyard
　　　do not have my advice and assistance.
　　　They are too weak and feeble and disorganised.
　　　They dote on her!

AGATHY: So you believe that between you and I,
　　　we can net her and bind her
　　　with the permanency of law.

　　　I have observed that she does speak with you.
　　　I hope you are telling her
　　　that I am a Greek god,
　　　even better than Ulysses.

PETROCULOS: What else could I be saying to her?
　　　Of course I tell her
　　　that Zeus gave birth to you.

I have explained to you
when we started to collaborate together,
that what I seek is the security of Ithaca
and the regions around it.
I am a law maker not a law breaker.
I believe in law and order,
and I am a civilised and educated man.

AGATHY: I am the only suitor worth her consideration.

PETROCULOS: I will offer her my counsel.
    And here is the plan, my boy.
    If she was going to choose you,
    she would have done this already.
    She is not going to betray the memory of Ulysses,
    and I don't even think she likes you—
    no offence to your high sexual drive.

    So you and I need to work together
    to obtain the wealth we want,
    since neither one of us
    cares for her or her son.

    I recommend and advise,
    —and I suggest you take it in,
    Son of Zeus—
    that you *frighten* her a little bit—
    put sexual pressure on her, but don't rape her;
    traumatise her, but don't bruise her.

    She will not reach out to any other suitors for assistance,
    so we are protected.
    She will come and find me, Agathy,
    and she will seek my services for the safety of her son.

    Of course, I will marry her but I will not bed her.
    You can have her
    or send her home to your family as a servant.

It will work.

When she feels threatened by you,
she will be drawn to me
for the safety and security of both herself and her son.
When she chooses me it will be
because I have told her that she can trust me
and that I will protect her and her son from all others.

AGATHY: And what do you want for your services?

PETROCULOS: I want the regions and some of Ithaca
under my orders and control.

AGATHY: You are right!
I have noticed that she heats up
when I follow her on her walks,
walks fast and tries to avoid me.

PETROCULOS: How do you know that she "heats up"?
And is the heating from the waist down
or the neck up?

AGATHY: I told you before,
I have made it my life's work to study women.
Of course she heats neck upwards
for her cheeks become red
and her hands are clenched.
I tell you she is hiding her deep desire for me.
I understand that she is baiting me
and playing the game of the vixen.
She wants to save face by not being too eager
to have me sexually.
I have seen her shake her head
and walk fast away from me.
Are you saying this is not
sexual attraction towards me?

PETROCULOS: Well, my boy,
    you've already done the hard work in getting her attention.

AGATHY: She . . . Quick, Petroculos! I can hear her steps!
    Leave her with me
    and I will show her what she is missing.

PETROCULOS: I will leave you alone with Penelope.
    Remember that the other men must not know
    of your physical aggression towards her.
    And for heaven's sake and for your life's sake,
    do not bruise her!

[AGATHY exits.]

PETROCULOS: Yes, you fool.
    Drive her into my arms.
    I will have Penelope legally
    and you will make sure that she trusts only me.

    For I will offer her my loyalty,
    my devotion and compassion, and my understanding.
    And I will offer myself to her as her loving, caring friend.
    I will seek to protect her son
    (until we are married, at least),
    and I will offer to her
    the love of her father, her brother, and her sister.
    In all our talks, she often refers to me
    as her sister.

    I will promise her to keep peace in the region,
    to legally remove the suitors,
    and allow her to wait for Ulysses.
    She would believe that a sister
    would allow her to wait for her husband.

    If and when he returns,
    I shall be happy for both of them.

And why should I be happy?
Because I love her in a platonic way.

She will choose me.
My age and wisdom will help me.
She will choose security and safety.

Yes, you fool!
Drive her into my arms
and then I will have you killed
for being too intimate
with my wifely sister.

[*PETROCULOS exits.*]

ACT V
THE SUITORS

Colours of the Forest

Scene 1 – The Wolf

[*AGATHY approaches PENELOPE as she walks towards him. She tries to walk away from him to escape into the forest, but he steps in front of her and she has to speak with him.*]

AGATHY: Penelope, I heard you in the garden
    and wanted to walk with you.

PENELOPE: I like to walk alone.

AGATHY: Dear Penelope, you do not have to be alone.
    Why are you tormenting yourself with this self-denial
    and not being with a man who can make you happy?
    I can make you happy.
    Being with me will remove
    this gloom and depression
    that travels with you.

PENELOPE: I am not *that* depressed.
    And if I suffered from this self-indulgence
    I would marry one of you
    so that I could torment you
    and make your life a living hell.
    In fact, I would marry *all* of you,
    so that you all could suffer from my depression.

AGATHY: Penelope, Penelope.
    My love, my dear one, my only one—

PENELOPE: Now I am feeling depressed.

AGATHY: I'm feeling excited by such talk.
　　Is this your foreplay?
　　All this and humour also!
　　My sweet little woman.

PENELOPE: Oh, but I was not humouring you, little man.

AGATHY: This is serious for me.
　　I know you like to play with my deep feelings for you,
　　and I will allow you some fun,
　　but I must talk with you.

　　Has anyone told you
　　that you are beautiful, truly beautiful?
　　I have been with many women,
　　so many that I have lost count,
　　but you are truly beautiful!

PENELOPE: Oh, do you really believe
　　after being surrounded by over a hundred suitors
　　that I not would hear such words from other men?
　　But they are empty words, to catch the fish,
　　to net the wild creature.
　　Only empty words.

AGATHY: My love, men are hunters and fishermen.
　　You are correct—they are baiting you.
　　But you must believe me when I say to you
　　that I have not
　　thought of any other woman
　　all the time I have been on your island.
　　All other women, compared to you,
　　look like my grandfather.

PENELOPE: Go and be with your grandfather.

AGATHY: Dear Penelope, my concern
　　　　is for you from the other men.
　　　　They are getting restless.

　　　　And for how long do you think
　　　　you will be able to call them brothers and fathers and sisters?
　　　　You need a strong man who will protect you
　　　　and send them back to their homes,
　　　　back to their mistresses.

PENELOPE: Please do not concern yourself
　　　　with my welfare and safety.

AGATHY: Does it not drive you mad
　　　　to have so many men around you and with you
　　　　and not sleep with any?
　　　　You sleep in an empty bed every night.

　　　　Where is Ulysses? Should he not have returned by now?
　　　　All the others have returned to their homes.
　　　　He has found someone else.
　　　　How can you continue to resist for so long
　　　　for a lie?
　　　　Aren't you like other women?
　　　　Aren't you wanting and longing?
　　　　Don't you lust for man?

PENELOPE: I have chosen this Journey,
　　　　and I have chosen to remain
　　　　faithful and devoted
　　　　to my heart, vision, and destiny.
　　　　Ulysses is alive!

　　　　And why he is not with me
　　　　is because something or someone
　　　　is preventing his return home.

But he will return!

Until he does,
I am not afraid to be alone in my bed.
I am not afraid to be alone with my thoughts.
And I am not afraid of abandonment and betrayal.
Betrayal is here.
Betrayal is all around us.

Look around you. Look in you.
It is all around you.

As for you, Agathy, you are a common species of man.
You work in a pack, as wolves do,
to achieve your ends.
I do not trust you.
I do not lust for you.
I do not want your company.

AGATHY: Come, Penelope my love,
      give up this madness.
      It is not healthy for you as a woman.
      You are playing with me
      so that I can come over and touch you,
      and you touch me.

PENELOPE: I would not touch you,
      let alone play with you.
      You do not understand.

      It is not about sex,
      it is about my mind, my heart, my spirit,
      desire, passion, and vision,
      my seeking, searching, longing.
      My longing for Ulysses
      and that he find his way home.

As for being alone, I sing to the sea,
and the sea carries the song to my husband.
The sea keeps my life afloat;
Therefore, we have an intimacy
that few would understand or want.

AGATHY: I have come at the right time in your life.
This morbid melancholy,
this foreign language that you speak,
this solitude that you live in,
it will drive you mad.
It will dry you up as a woman.

PENELOPE: You know nothing about women's fluids,
and you are starting to make me angry.

AGATHY: My dear Penelope, to be a little wild is exciting,
but to be so unrestricted, unbridled,
and unharnessed is frightening.
You cannot live the rest of your life on the past.
I will not allow you.

PENELOPE: How can it be the past
when it prevents you from having what you want
in the present and the future?

How can it be the past
when every moment, every thought and action,
is alive and electric with the substance of Ulysses?

My lover is not of the past;
he is of the present and now
and I have the seeds of his soul and body
under my tongue and in the wilderness of my soul.

When I am surrounded by aloneness and darkness
I bite on these seeds from eternity
and I am no longer afraid or alone.

He is swimming in me.
He lives; he lives in me.

Are you so blinded
by your own ambitions and vanity
that you do not see Ulysses swimming in me?

How can that be the past?
He is in the heat of the moment,
he is in the fire of yesterday
and he is of the spark of tomorrow.

He is in front of me, preventing your claim on me.
He is behind me, preventing your betrayal of me.
He is inside me
and keeps me alive
and passionately in love.

AGATHY: When you speak like that, Penelope, you frighten me.
How will you ever settle
into a calm and domesticated relationship with me?

Let me help you and your son.
Real people do not love as you say.
These are poems from poets who make things up.
Such people have invented love
because the world is too barren and lonely for them.
They suffer from anomalies
because of the long hours and years in living alone.

I see you have been speaking
with the old men who dote on you.
I don't know why they came here.
Maybe just to get away from family and relatives.

PENELOPE: Or demanding mistresses?

AGATHY: The old men.
Did they come here to seduce you or to nurse you?

What is it about you and older men?
The older they are, the more time you spend with them.

PENELOPE: They are impotent—or so they tell me.
What they lust for is prestige and power
rather than sexual satisfaction.
Do you think you will be saying that you are impotent
when you get to their age?

AGATHY: Never!
I suppose you are going to tell me
that one gains wisdom in life
when one can no longer light the fire of the body.
I think you are shrewd,
cunning, and clever,
and you have seduced
the only thing that still works—their minds.

PENELOPE: Well no one can accuse me
of seducing your mind.
It would mean that I would have to find it first.

AGATHY: Penelope. You do make me suffer.
But I think you enjoy the little suffering
and the little deaths that you inflict on me.
I am happy to suffer this for you,
for you will choose me in the end.
You will be pleading with me to help you.

PENELOPE: You don't understand
that once you have experienced
this love from the absolute,
you can never be with anyone else.
To have experienced soul immortality,
the seed from eternity,
it is this that you and lover
are always connected to in absence.

Ulysses is here.
Can't you see him in my eyes?
Can't you see him on my body?
Can't you hear him in my voice?

Ulysses is here because he has never left me.
When I sleep he is next to me,
when I awake he plays with me
and while I am talking to you
he is shaking his head and saying,
"Why are you wasting your time with such a fool?"

AGATHY: Penelope. Stop this madness.
You are not going to frighten me
with your ravings that Ulysses is here.

PENELOPE: How could you stand it
to want to be with me
when you know that I would only see Ulysses?
What type of man does that?

AGATHY: One who has weighed all the benefits and profits
from marrying the beautiful Penelope.
A sane man.

PENELOPE: Why have you decided
to settle for so little, Agathy?
The next question that follows this logic is:
how good are you sexually
when you are willing to settle with the fact
that Ulysses would be in your bed?

AGATHY: You go on and on, just like a woman
who has been given too much freedom
for your own good.
And you are constant
in your defiance and rejection of all
and run threads around the thinking of a simple man.

I can see by your smile that you think me simple?
I know this: that you will have to choose me.
It will be I who you will choose
when all the others start to show you their fangs and claws,
as they grow weary with waiting
for the elusive and cunning Penelope.

There will be no Ulysses to rescue you.
Your son will be killed.
You can barely keep him alive
with your poor excuses.

And while you are eating away at the time
that is running out for you,
they are all pretending,
hiding their claws and fangs
until you step out of the law.
Time will seal you to the law of the land.
Time will seal you to me.

PENELOPE: I will choose my husband to the end.
I chose him in the beginning
and I choose my husband Ulysses, *now*.

AGATHY: He will not hear you.
He will not come.
The man you will take to bed will be me.

I have watched you
and smelled your sweetness as you pass.
I have looked at you from a distance
and you are preoccupied with your devotion.
Well, devote yourself to me, I am here.
I am here, Ulysses is absent.

It makes no difference to me.
I don't want what you have in your mind or heart.
I want what you have here.

[*AGATHY touches PENELOPE'S genital area and proceeds to kiss her.*
He forces her to kiss him, but it goes horribly wrong
for he is struggling to remove himself from her mouth.
PENELOPE puts her hands on his head and holds him
while he is struggling to get away from her
Finally PENELOPE lets go and there is blood around his mouth.
He falls to his knees, wipes his mouth, and then stands. PENELOPE
wipes his blood from her mouth.]

PENELOPE: I swear by the love that makes and breaks me,
if you ever come near me again,
if you ever try to touch me again,
I will cut you while you sleep.
I will make sure I use the same instruments
that we use for our horses.
I will cut away from you
all your generations to come,
and feed them to my hounds.

[*AGATHY runs from her wiping his mouth, which is covered with blood.*
He is visibly shaken by her response to his sexual advances]

Scene 2 – The Jackal

[*PENELOPE is still standing in the same place.*
PETROCULOS comes running from the side of the stage to her.]

PETROCULOS: What is that noise?
What is going on?
Penelope, are you alright?

PENELOPE: Oh, my dear friend, Petroculos!
What would I do without your concern?

PETROCULOS: What happened?
I was walking so that I could clear my head

and I heard your voice and a man's voice,
and I was not sure.
I ran as fast as I could, to see if you were all right.
You have some blood on your lips!
Here let me wipe it off for you.

[*PENELOPE refuses and wipes it off with her hand.*]

PENELOPE: Agathy tried to convince me
that he was the man for me.

PETROCULOS: Here, let me hold you.

PENELOPE: Do you think that by holding me
it will remove from me this experience?
No, I do not want to be comforted
or sedated from what I feel.
I want to rage so that next time he comes near me
I will fulfil my promise to him.

I will not be unsexed by any man.
And if any man tries to brand me as his,
I swear by all that makes and breaks me
I will cut him while he sleeps.
All enemies have to sleep,
and that is when you bleed them
and drain them from their manhood, or their life.

PETROCULOS: Such rage. Was it as bad as that?
The brute—I will deal with him later,
if one can deal with him.

But I am concerned about you.
Things have changed in Ithaca.
The suitors have become bored
and tired and sexually frustrated
waiting for your decision.
I knew that it would come to this.

Agathy has become restless
and will not follow the ways of the law.
You do know he has an army
waiting to hear from him
so that they can come and attack Ithaca.

I don't know if any of us here has the ability
to stop the chain of events once they start.
There will be much bloodshed.
But I am not concerned about their blood;
I am concerned about you and your son.

PENELOPE: What can I do to save my son?
I have kept him safe all these years.
I will not have him slaughtered.
I would rather die than see this happen.

But before I surrender my sword
I will send a few of the suitors to Hades
to find their legal wives.

PETROCULOS: Dear Penelope, how difficult it must be for you,
to have all of us here for so long.
We have become locusts and intruders in your home.
I have been thinking about this situation.
It really cannot continue.

PENELOPE: What do you suggest, my trusted friend?
I always believe in outwitting and out-planning the enemy.

PETROCULOS: One must always keep above and below
the nets they throw.
A warrior of courage and discipline
uses his sword only when they have netted him.

PENELOPE: My sword is the last act of defence
to save my son's life.
What can I do to keep my son alive

and safe from the dangers
that come with me and his father?

PETROCULOS: I will give you some suggestions,
but the choice will have to be yours and yours alone.

First, I want to tell you
how I marvel at how you have kept you and your son alive
for so long
with so many vultures and invaders
waiting and waiting for you to trip up,
or make a mistake,
or simply give in and give up.

Truly, Penelope, you are a great diplomat.

And the tapestry was a brilliant idea,
for it gave you more time for Ulysses's return
to conduct yourself as a woman of integrity
following the law of the land.

Now let me see if I can offer you some advice
in which you do not compromise
your position and standing.
We all have followed the law of the land,
but the time is coming that this law will be useless
in the face of conquest and brute force.

Laws do not exist when there is chaos and violence.
Each man makes his own law
and murder is part of their law.

On the other hand, I have always been here for you.
I have even advised you
on the weakness of certain men
and how to avoid them
and protect yourself from their advances
without hurting their vanity.

I have always told all of them to follow the law
and to respect you and your son.

PENELOPE: Yes, Petroculos.
You have proven yourself more than once
a fair man in the face of turbulence and chaos.

PETROCULOS: Dear Penelope, your time is running out.
You will have to choose soon,
and from the struggle I heard
that you had with Agathy,
your decision or your conquest is very near.

Agathy is the strongest here
and he does have a small army
waiting to support him when he is ready to strike.
We all have small armies waiting at the port of Ithaca.

You may avoid conquest
and the murder of your son
if you marry me.

PENELOPE: It will be a marriage of convenience,
for I only see you as my sister.

PETROCULOS: Very few marriages have to do with love.
It is about two people seeking security and protection
from the invasion of the outside world.
They combine their skills and territories
and have a better place in the world
because they have more assets and power
and can live in security, comfort, and safety.

So you see, my dear Penelope,
our marriage would offer you all the above.
Marry me, Penelope.

I know you do not love me,
and I am not in love with you.

You are too sensible and disciplined
for such wild flights and fancies of the heart and passion.

I am talking about a marriage of convenience
in which I can offer you safety and protection.
If you do not choose me, I cannot protect you
because all the men have the right of the law to you.
You belong to all of us
and no one will leave this island
until you choose a husband.

PENELOPE: Are you telling me
that if I chose you as my husband
all the others will leave and my son will be safe?

PETROCULOS: Poor, hunted, tormented Penelope.
I have told you from the beginning,
I only came to Ithaca so that there is no bloodshed
and to keep peace in the region.
And I wanted to keep you safe.

PENELOPE: I cannot make this decision at this moment,
I need time to think.
I cannot compromise
the truth and love of my heart.
What of Ulysses? I love Ulysses.
How can I enter a marriage of convenience with you?
What of my love?

PETROCULOS: Ulysses, if he returns,
will understand that you had no other choice.
Besides, I will set you free
to be with your first husband.

Remember, we will not marry for love
but rather that you do not wake to find Agathy
or any other lustful suitor in your bed
and your poor dear son murdered.

PENELOPE: Thank you my dear friend,
for concerning yourself with my son's protection
and my welfare and safety.

I will think about what you have suggested
and I will speak with you further about this.
I can sense the stillness and restlessness
and you may well be right,
for my tapestry is nearly finished.

[*PENELOPE exits.
PETROCULOS speaks his thoughts.*]

PETROCULOS: [*to himself*] Penelope, you are smelling the bait for
your trap.
Soon you will come into it
and I will spring it shut on you.
We will marry. You will have no choice.

I will stir the hearts of the other men.
I will stir their doubts and I will enrage them
over you tricking them with the tapestry.
You will be forced to choose
or be conquered by all of us.

Penelope, you will marry me.
I will have to put Agathy to death
for his improper sexual advances towards you.
The other suitors will leave Ithaca,
and I will send you to my home
as a gift to my family—as a servant.

At some time in the future,
you and your poetic son
will join Ulysses on the sea.
We will find your drowned bodies.
I will grieve for this loss of you, my wife,
and the loss of Telemachus,

since the world will believe I loved him,
as the son I never had.

I will gain Ithaca and the regions around for trade
and I will be a most respected
and reverenced senior leader,
one who will not be questioned
when others leave me to the personal tragedy
of losing my wife.

As for Ulysses, if he does come back
he will have to face Penelope's betrayal,
the loss of his son, and my army
will quickly put the spear of departure to his heels.

What a catastrophe!
Three wasted lives!
But the three deaths will make my life permanent
in privileges and wealth.
I will be powerful, respected, and admired.

The world will say, "Look at noble Petroculos.
He has lost so much.
Life has been unkind to him
and yet he continues to conduct himself
with human integrity
and the actions of a selfless man
in the service of his country."

ACT VI
TELEMACHUS

Colours of Twilight

[TELEMACHUS *is a young man, about twenty-five, tall and graceful. He has his mother's auburn hair and light skin, with piercing blue eyes. He is soft spoken and gives the appearance of being thoughtful and learned in the arts of music, poetry, and philosophy. He enters his mother's chambers: the secret room, which the suitors have not seen, the chambers that belong to Penelope and Ulysses with the tree and the carvings. PENELOPE is at her tapestry. TELEMACHUS enters.*]

TELEMACHUS: Mother, how can you stay at that tapestry
    when there is so much uncertainty in our lives?

PENELOPE: Life is certain. Death is certain.
    It is the ways of man
    and the way he conducts himself
    that bring about uncertainty, not only to his life
    but to all other lives around him.

    It is man who brings uncertainty
    with his conquest and domination,
    the controlling and confinement
    of all other lives around him.

    How do you dispense uncertainty?
    You think, you organise.
    You plan and you act in the face of uncertainty.
    You affirm life, my son.
    Say *yes* to life.
    The uncertainty that you speak about
    becomes a cancer that destroys
    the passion and affirmation in a man.

TELEMACHUS: What do you want me to do?
    All these years you have been preoccupied
    with these threads that you put in during the day
    and undo at night.
    I have seen you embroider my father's ship
    on the canvas during the day
    only to see you undo it at night.

PENELOPE: I sail with him at night,
    and during the day I hide him from others.

TELEMACHUS: I do not know what to do.
    I fear to act and I fear not to act.
    Whichever way I decide
    will bring turmoil and further uncertainty.

PENELOPE: These past ten years it is this tapestry
    and my desire to do the right thing for my lost husband,
    for your shipwrecked father,
    that has given us more time.

    I have conducted myself
    as a woman of the law
    and that is why those out there
    have not broken the law with violence or murder.

TELEMACHUS: But they will break the law!
    We do not have much time.
    The hunters have thrown the net
    of our captivity.

    You have managed to find something
    within the law
    that has given us more time,
    but not anymore.

    We have run out of threads,
    and the men outside

are coiling and coiling
the black thread of our fate
around and around our ankles,
and they will pull and pull
until we fall.

Our time is running out.

PENELOPE: I sense it too.
I see the net of our captivity becoming tighter;
our world is getting smaller.

TELEMACHUS: I know you cannot agree to marry any of them.
They are wolves, wild dogs, and jackals.
They all want to steal what belongs to Ulysses.
Those men out there want to hunt and kill you.
They haven't driven you insane,
or maybe that will be the last lie
that they invent about you, mother—
that you have gone insane
with your longing and grief for my father,
and therefore they had to take over our region.

PENELOPE: They will not declare me mad
because they want to show to the world
that they have married a sane woman.
They want me sane.
As Agamemnon wanted the cunning intellect of your father,
these men want my intellect and prestige.
They will not declare me mad.
I am their prize.

TELEMACHUS: They will kill you after they have wed you.

PENELOPE: I will not wed any of them.
It has never been a moral right,
or a right within the law, that they be here.

TELEMACHUS: Mother, beloved mother. They are pulling in the nets!

PENELOPE: My son you must leave.

TELEMACHUS: Leave without you?
     The one who has kept me alive and sane all these years?
     The one who has planned and plotted
     against the armies of conquerors
     with only your determination
     and those cursed and blessed threads.

     I could never leave you!

PENELOPE: You must leave.
     You must harden your heart
     and abandon me to my fate.

TELEMACHUS: I will not do this,
     not even for you, mother.
     I love you, and I will not abandon you
     in the crisis of our lives.

     I do not have this metal will or stone heart.
     What you ask me to do
     takes a different kind of ruthless courage.
     I do not have such courage.

     I am caught mother,
     like a freshly caught creature.
     And all the tensions of uncertainty
     pull like hooks in my chest.

     I am caught and I cannot act,
     for whatever way I act
     it will bring betrayal and death.

     Tell me, mother,
     was my father a great warrior?

PENELOPE: Yes, he was,
    and he taught me the skill of the sword
    to protect you or him in such a critical time.
    Yes, your father was such a man who would strike,
    and yes he was stained with other men's blood.

TELEMACHUS: I love my father,
    but I do not have his heart
    to pick up a sword and fight.

    I question and seek what is hidden from me.
    I am continually in the quest
    to find the missing parts of me in the hidden.
    My actions are uncertain
    because my heart loves
    and cannot take the life of another.

    All my actions suffer from this sadness in my heart.
    And therefore I miss my target.
    I was an archer in life,
    but I missed my target, Mother.

PENELOPE: You will leave and you will leave tonight.

TELEMACHUS: If I left, you will be killed
    by whoever you choose.
    If I stay, we both will be killed.

    I will probably be the sacrifice on your wedding.
    My blood will stain your marriage bed.

    I can't leave you alone in this crisis,
    and at the same time I cannot protect you.
    I have thought about this, Mother.
    I have spent many nights awake,
    soaking in my sweat at our fate and final outcome.

I cannot leave you.

PENELOPE: Go and search for your father.
If I am to die at the hands of either the wolf or jackal,
I would rather die knowing
that you have escaped their nets.

Your father did not have a choice.
Either he went or all of us would have been killed.
You must learn to depend on your intuition,
your intellect, and your blood affirmation.

My son, my son.

You will leave and you will leave tonight.
I am begging you. [*drops to her knees*]
I am on my knees. Save yourself.
You are all truth and beauty to me.
Save this seed in you
and leave me to my choices and fate.

TELEMACHUS: No, no, no! I will not leave!
And as the blade falls,
I will see my father and you welcoming me home.

[*They hold each other and weep.*]

PENELOPE: It has come to this.
I plead with you, my son.
You can only save me by saving yourself.
You must leave and find your father and his men.
You must organise to take back
what these men seem to have made their own,
because they have found a back door in the law.

TELEMACHUS: I have thought many times
to cut them with my sword while they slept:
one by one, the young, and the old.
When I pick up my father's sword,

such a weight and burden comes upon my soul,
and I freeze. Mother, I freeze—
not with fear or doubt
but with the knowledge that this blade
has gutted and disembowelled the lives of other men.

And yet . . . although I realise
that I would be in the right to kill them in their sleep,
I do not have the might to spill another man's blood
into the thirsty earth.

And I well realise
that I cannot kill them while they are awake.
I do not have their training, age, or skill.

I question the structure of appearance
and the shifting and changing masks
of the taught things.

I question my place and role in all this disaster.

PENELOPE: Listen, I can hear noises outside.
Are they organising themselves?
I will give my answer to Petroculos,
to gain some more time while you escape.

TELEMACHUS: Do you mean to tell me
that you will marry this man?
He is a jackal.
I have watched him with the others.

He always speaks wisely and yet
seeks every opportunity to gain power for himself.
He has become friends with Agathy.
I have more than once seen them talking together.

I do not think they are speaking
about poetry or philosophy
and since they have nothing in common,

they are probably planning our fate together.

If you choose Petroculos, we are dead.
He will arrange an accident for us.

PENELOPE: I choose my husband Ulysses in life.
I choose Ulysses in death.

TELEMACHUS: Petroculos is planning something.
He is not going to wait anymore.
How did you manage to stay alive so long?
Have you never suffered fear?

PENELOPE: I suffer from the inquisition of my soul.
I suffer from fear of not being able to keep you alive.
This fear is with me all the time.
My desire is to keep you alive.
I do not fear these men's betrayals.

They cannot remove what is mine or of me.
The worst thing a man can do in his life
is not to have lived it,
and you can only live your life by being in it,
facing all your struggles and fears,
and then—Telemachus—asking for more.

The deeper you get, the more you find of yourself.
The more you live in safety and security
—the world of mediocrity—
the less you have of what gives meaning to life:
deep longing and deep love.

You listen to me: whatever happens here
—and expect the worst—
you *will* leave.

TELEMACHUS: I will not leave you here alone.
And yet you cannot come with me.
I am torn between you and my father,

and I cannot act.
I must wait and see what will happen.

PENELOPE: All victims of war wait
    to see what will happen
    and hope that they will be spared.
    We will not be spared,
    and we will not wait to see what will happen.

TELEMACHUS: I must wait for my father.
    In the first ten years of his departure from our lives
    I grieved and ached to see his face
    and to feel his reassurance
    that life will return him to us, to each other.

    Life did not return him after ten years.
    He did not return to us.
    Instead we had a plague of men
    who have sought the region and you.
    And here have they stayed.

    Now they are ready to claim illegally and legally
    what they think is rightfully theirs.
    I tell you, Mother, they will want blood for their wait.

    The one you choose will want my blood and later yours.
    The others you did not choose will also seek blood.
    I feel like a fly caught in the net of the spider.

PENELOPE: You are not a fly, you are a man,
    and you are in your life
    and therefore able to take the sword.

    [*Grasps and holds her son by his shirt.*]
    I love you, my son.
    What will happen unless you act
    is that you will be killed. And worse for me.

They will make me watch your death,
as they will make you watch
my humiliation and violation.

We are not going to sit here waiting for them to kill us.
Bring me my sword. It is time for war.
A wise man will not seek war,
but when it comes to him,
and all reason has vanished,
then it is time
to cut the destroyers of life with a hot blade.

I am not going to offer you as a sacrifice.
As for me, I will know life
in knowing you have escaped.
It is not your time to die.
This is not the time for you.

Now leave me, my son.
Head to the sea.
There will be a vessel waiting
to take you away from me and Ithaca.

[*They embrace.*]

TELEMACHUS: Is it true, what the masters say,
that "men's souls are sinister and black
and the world will always burn with fire and weapons"?[38]

I am not leaving you, Mother.
I am not leaving. [*kisses his mother*]

PENELOPE: My beautiful son, we have hurt the world.
We have hurt you.
My beautiful son, I could not bear
to not see you for all eternity.

[*They both embrace and weep
More noises are heard outside, men screaming, running, things breaking.*]

PENELOPE: Bring my sword.

    No one will touch you while I live.

    Bring my sword.

    Let me look outside.

[Both go to look outside.
The noises stop and there are only moans of pain.]

ACT VII
THE RETURN

Colours of Dawn

TELEMACHUS: Mother, mother!
　　I can see a beggar coming towards us.
　　There is something that is familiar about him.

PENELOPE: Let me look. It is probably a trick.
　　You can't believe in the appearance of things.

TELEMACHUS: Our dog knows him.
　　He has removed his beggar clothes and has a sword.
　　Mother! He is stained in blood.
　　And mother, the lazy and fat suitors are not moving.
　　They are all lying still.

[Much noise and yelling is heard outside.]

PENELOPE: Telemachus, let me look.
　　I cannot see what you see;
　　it is too dark and too many things,
　　and people are broken outside this door.

　　When this man comes here, you be ready.
　　No indecision, for it will cost us
　　our choice on how we will die.
　　No hesitation.

　　My sword will be ready to strike and strike hard.

TELEMACHUS: I sense him to be my father.
　　I smell the sameness of his blood.

PENELOPE: My son, you were not made for war.
    You have the soul of a poet
    who seeks refuge in the world of love.
    My world and your father's world has been of love,

    and then the world found us
    and caught us in its net,
    and we became hunters and the hunted,
    and still we kept the teachings
    of the fool and the lover alive.

    Get ready, to hold, hold the last breath.
    How sweet life is at the end,
    how sweet it is in the beginning.

    Get beside me and stay there
    for when his sword clashes with mine
    he will not aim for you.
    If you want love to remain in this world
    then you will have to protect it.

                    [*TELEMACHUS pick up a sword and weeps.*]

TELEMACHUS: I cannot kill. I cannot protect you.
    I cannot protect myself.
    The ways of the world are not my ways,
    and I am ready to leave as I was ready yesterday.

    Mother, you have taught me many things
    and my most loved teaching of yours
    is longing, deep longing.

    I cannot kill another.
    You taught me to worship and reverence life.
    I cannot kill this old man.
    He reminds me too much of my father. [*sobs*]

PENELOPE: My son, it is your father and I
    who are damned for allowing others

to deceive us into following a war we did not invent,
to allow others to reward us for killing.

As you cannot kill, I cannot do otherwise—I will protect you.

You do not disappoint me, my son.
You are different.
You have gone further,
and may your father and I become your bridge
that will get you across the abyss
and darkness of our world.

We have different responsibilities in love, in life.
Mine is to protect you
and yours is to remain tender
and free from spilling blood.

[*The stranger comes on stage. He is dressed as an old beggar. He is older twenty years, since PENELOPE has last seen him, and he is unrecognisable because of his unkempt appearance. He is covered in blood. His body language speaks of humility that time and loss has taught him. He has long, unkempt hair and a beard that is grey. But he is still a strong man. PENELOPE holds her sword ready for battle. TELEMACHUS is beside her. He realises who the stranger is and runs to him.*]

TELEMACHUS: Father, Father, Father!
I knew it was you!

[*PENELOPE is still holding her sword, trying to pull her son away from the embrace of the stranger.*]

ULYSSES: My son, my son, how beautiful you have grown!
I am told you have not spilled blood like the rest of us.
Your mother has kept your mind and hands
clean from this insanity,
this plague of spiritual decay.
The insanity of foaming dogs,

the wolves, the jackals,
the collectors, the hunters
that see other men's lives
no more than that of insects.
Insects that they must exterminate.

My son, my son, I am ashamed for what I have done
and for what I have allowed other men
to influence me to do
in the name of gain, profit
and a better world, and the spread
of our civilisation.
Be wary of those who want to change the world
with the spilling of other men's blood.

[*ULYSSES weeps as he tries to wipe the blood off his son's clothes.*]

I have stained you with other men's blood.
I have filled your young life
with so much betrayal and human blood.

PENELOPE: Who are you?
[*She circles him with her sword still ready for battle.*]
Take your hands off my son.
He is innocent and believes the truth and the lies.

[*ULYSSES moves forward to PENELOPE.*
She puts the sword between them.]

ULYSSES: My wife, my love, my lost and found life!
Don't you remember me?
Have I aged so much
that you do not remember me?
I have not forgotten you.
I have always seen your face in front of me.

The sirens had your face
and they even took on your voice

to try to trick me not to return to you.

All my strength, all my planning,
all my scheming has gone into returning home.
All my waking and sleeping moments
have been filled with wanting,
longing, aching to return to you.

PENELOPE: You keep your distance.
You look like my husband.
Let me see the cut on your knee.
[ULYSSES shows her the cut on his knee.]
Yes, you have that. But that is not enough.

This could be another trick.
You could be evil in disguise.
I am not going to put down my sword,
and unless you have something
more intimate to say about my husband
prepare yourself to battle with me.

No! Because you are playing the cruellest trick on me,
prepare to die!

ULYSSES: Penelope!
[He kneels in front of her and puts down his sword at her feet.]
I am your husband.
It is right that you be sceptical of all
who call themselves your friend, lover, or husband.
I am Ulysses, returned to bring peace and freedom
to you and my home.

I carved for you, your bedhead.
I remember you wanted the forest,
rivers and even the pebbles
carved on our bedhead.

You wanted the tree to remain in the ground
so that it would remain living.
This tree will live as our love does,
and when we have died this tree
will hold us in its roots together.

You told me how the tree
keeps the world together with its roots
and how it gathers the dreams of the heavens
and brings them to us in its breath.
You told me how you believed
that a tree is like a great person
that holds many life forms in it and on it,
the tree where many can find shelter,
dreams and vision.

You told me the tree is your home,
and when I could not be with you,
the tree would bring you my dreams from the sky.
In our youth you were the fire in my soul.
In our old age, you are the inspiration in my heart.

I have returned to find you divinely accomplished,
beautiful in your wisdom and strength.
My beautiful wife, my passionate lover,
I have returned to you.
I am now complete.
You may strike with your sword or love me in our bed.

[*PENELOPE places the sword besides ULYSSES and drops to her
knees with him.*]

ACT VIII
WHISPERS

Colours of Sunset

"This only is denied to God: the ability to undo the past."[39]

[The haunting and death of Ulysses, the whispers of the dead. PENELOPE and ULYSSES are together. The other voices are heard as a reaction to their conversation. It is a haunting. It is the decisions that ULYSSES has made in the past. They actually have an entity and voices of the different people from the past that move between, in and out of their thoughts and conversation with each other. These are the signs that ULYSSES is in the transition of his physical death.

ASTYNAX: Hector's murdered young son. Ulysses had an influence in the final decision to throw the boy from the Trojan walls to his death.

ANDROMACHE: Mother of Astynax

SIREN: Ulysses was the only one that heard the song of the sirens. He never spoke about it to anyone, but the song of the sirens has never left him, and it returns with the other phantoms of his life. He never told anyone what she sounded like or what she told him.

DESTINY has Ulysses's face and voice. In the classical literature and philosophies it was believed that all the decisions we make eventually become our destiny; therefore, destiny has the face of the core of our very nature: it has our face because it is us that have made all our decisions and arrived at our destination. This occurs at the end of man's life, and there is nothing he can do to change his past actions, simply because he has no more energy or time in his life, and simply because you cannot bring the dead back, or the past to change it.

It is clear that Ulysses, even though he is a tragic character, has made decisions that have caused destruction and the death of a young child. In this part of his life

133

and death all meet up, and all voice their grief and pain. Ulysses cannot escape this on his death bed, nor does he want to escape it.[40]

The SIREN approaches him: a beautiful woman, similar to Penelope as the sirens took on the image of the one we love the most.]

SIREN: Ulysses, I am the siren who opened your heart
    and saw all your secrets,
    all the deep longing,
    and all the dark ambitions.

    You thought you were safe from my song,
    like your men whose ears were stuffed with wax.
    You were tied to the rails of your vessel.
    I found you and I have travelled with you
    and will travel with you.

    You and you alone have made me yours.
    Why have you not spoken about me to Penelope?
    Is this the one infidelity that you have not shared with her?
    I know you love me
    and that is why you have never spoken about me to anyone.

    Why did you not stay on the sea with me?
    Why did you not stay with me?
    You love me enough
    to have brought me to your bed with Penelope.
    And when you have made love to her,
    who do you see: her or me?
    Who do you long for: her or me?

    For I am the image and substance
    of the young Penelope before life
    and the weight of years and suffering
    aged the Penelope that shares your bed now.

    You might say you love her more
    because of her loyal character,

but you still lust for me.
Don't feel torn, Ulysses:
we are the same woman.

You should not have tried to outwit the laws
that are not written by man,
the laws that govern man,
the laws that hold everything
in suspension and in balance.
I am here with you now,
in the birth of your death.

[*DESTINY enters. He looks and is the young ULYSSES. He comes close to ULYSSES and there ULYSSES stares deeply into the eyes of his DESTINY, the DESTINY he made with his decisions, the DESTINY that has his face, his teeth, his fingerprints. The man looks deeply into ULYSSES.*]

DESTINY: You can call me Destiny, Ulysses.
I am your destiny.
You moulded me to fit you.
I am from the core of your nature,
what you took from the world,
what you shaped in the world,
what you killed in the world,
what you gave to the world.

I am all your life on this earth;
I am all your actions.
Have you remained faithful to your path,
to your journey?
Did you risk yourself on the journey of life,
or did you cut deep into your heart,
or the heart of another?

Did your choices follow you through your life?
Did you make your choices on vanity and arrogance?
Did they become your yoke of necessity?
Did you bury the truth and invent your own?

Did you choose to conquer?
Did you want fame and wealth?

Did you stop to think
that for every privilege you took for yourself,
someone else had to go without?

Do you remember your wars
and how many men you killed and why?
Was it really self-survival, or was it something more?
Lands? Armies? Wealth? Honour? Fame?

Do you remember Troy?

[ASTYNAX, *a young child of about ten, enters Ulysses's room: a beautiful,
blond-haired boy, glowing with the promise of a full life. He goes to ULYSSES
and takes his hand. ULYSSES recognises this child and trembles.*]

DESTINY: Do you remember this child, Ulysses?

ULYSSES: It is Hector's son, Astynax.

ASTYNAX: I can see you, Ulysses, crossing the river,
        but this time you do not have a boat
        and there are so many unnamed creatures
        swimming in the river.
        I have waited for you, Ulysses.

        You, who dashed and broke my young life.
        You, who returned me to darkness.

        I have waited for you
        to return you to the other shore,
        the other life, the unseen one,
        where men do not kill children
        and they do not conquer to accumulate,
        for they are not lacking in anything in the other life.

They watch the actions of the living
and shake their heads in disbelief
and say, "If only some had told me not to do that."

Is that how you feel now, Ulysses?
In this world there are layers of different people.
Some are under the earth
and lick the human blood that man spills without thought.
We call them furies.

There are those that sit quietly in the shadows
and suffer great sadness
for all the things they have not done,
for all the things that they have done:
we call them neither dead nor living.

There are those that we cannot find or see
in our transparent and invisible world.

There are the ones that have lived their lives,
and have been in their lives,
and have conducted themselves
in balance with the laws of the living and the dead.
They have not transgressed,
or gone beyond the doors inscribed with:
"all who enter here abandon all hope."[41]

We sometimes feel them
on the wings of the birds
or in the flicker of light.

I could not move beyond and above into the wings.
I needed and wanted to face you, Ulysses.

Will you be gone another twenty years?
There is no time in the other world.
Have you gone to conquer another Troy?
Or has life conquered you?

Have you gone to save a world, any world,
in exchange for the one that you burned to the ground?

I am the child who was murdered in Troy
You voted for me to be dropped from the walls of Troy,
and there I fell and broke into a million pieces.
I have come here
to guide you back into the Wooden Horse,
the Wooden House you thought about and devised
to trick and conquer the weary, embattled Trojans.

From that Wooden Horse
at night you entered our beds while we were asleep
and murdered all of us—
children, women, old men, young men—
and I was left alone, with only my grandmother, Hecuba.
You took my mother from me for your servant.
You could not let me live,
I being the son of the most noble man, Hector,
and you thought of another clever plan—
"See if the child can fly!"

I sense you wandering and searching
to change things
among the rivers of blood.
You would change things now, would you not?
And here our human frailty begins and ends.
We cannot change the past.
Agathon says, "This only is denied to God:
the ability to undo the past."[42]

[ANDROMACHE, *a tall noblewoman, enters the room dressed in mourning
clothes. Her hair is long and golden, like that of ASTYNAX, and her skin is pale.
Her face is gentle and kind. She is the mother of ASTYNAX.*]

ANDROMACHE: My child, I can hear you.
    I have been able to hear you,
    but I could not see you until this moment.

I wanted to reach you and could not.
Give me your hand or at least your little finger.

Dear child, so young in my arms,
so precious.
How well I remember the smell of your skin.

How well I remember our parting,
a parting that cut my life in half.
I was no longer in life.
What happened to me afterwards did not bother me.
I could not cry as I had no more tears in me.
I could not laugh, I could not love, I could not live.
And yet live I did, and I carried my body around,
weighted down by the coffin I live in.

Dear child, my life stopped when you lost your life.

ASTYNAX: Mother, sweet mother,
at last I can see you.
So long I could hear you,
I could smell you,
but I could not see you,
I could not touch you.

Mother, hold me.
I have missed you for all eternity.

Look, mother, look at Ulysses.
Isn't he a man full of regret?

ANDROMACHE: My precious child,
you are still loving the world.
You are still wanting to do good,
even to the murderer of your life
who stands motionless across me.

Look at him.
He doesn't look like a fearless warrior now, does he?

What is the matter, Ulysses?
Can't you out trick, outwit, break the laws of this law?
Look at you, Ulysses.

Look at what you have reduced my son to:
a shadow to be seen only by the dying.
Look at what you have reduced my life to:
a shadow in another shadow.
And look at what you have reduced your life to.

ULYSSES: Astynax, what can I do for you?

ANDROMACHE: You can give him back his life,
let him grow into a man,
let him know of love and let him die from old age.

What is the matter, Ulysses?
You, who defied the gods.
You, who thought you defeat and beat all.
You, who could outwit and outfox the fox.

Here you stand, knowing
you are at the hands of something
bigger and greater than you.

You are in the laws of life and death,
and you cannot move forward or backward.
You are helpless, as my son was.
You are helpless like I was.
You are helpless.

ULYSSES: I am here and I am accountable to all of you.
I draw you all into me.
I have searched and ached
for this wreckage of my life,
for the wreckage that I made out of your lives.
I have two marriages:
one of love and the other of blood,

and the blood has drowned me and consumed me.

The armies of those I love,
the armies of those I have driven into the ground,
consume me and engulf me
and in turn I have engulfed them.

They will not let me be until I go with them,
respond to them.
And I charge them full with the force
of my passing and coming life;
they charge into me.

And here we both are found,
locked in a struggle:
neither one winning, neither one losing.
Now I can hear.

When I was in full life
I was deaf to the suffering of others.
Now I can hear

"the splashing of tears,
the measureless rivers of human tears,"[43]
tears that I have caused—

and for what?

What am I taking with me in my other journey?
Nothing.
Nothing.
Nothing.

What have I left in kindness, in generosity?
Who will remember me?
Children and inexperienced men
that marvel at the conquests of war
and think me a hero

because I had a powerful army with me,
because I caught the enemy asleep and slaughtered them.

But no one will go into the life of the slain and butchered,
as if they did not matter in the scheme of things.
Now, in my last moments on this earth,
I can truly see with my own eyes
and with the eyes of those that I have destroyed.

SIREN: Ulysses, Ulysses, I kept you safe on the sea.
Return to the sea

DESTINY: He cannot escape me.
I am him and he is me.
We have a division within us.
I am the anchor of his nature,
the outcome of his choices,
the outcomes he did not want to face,
the compass of his human journey.
All he has touched in love or violence
will now seek and collide into him.
He seeks and collides into them
with the full force of his body and heart.

[ULYSSES falls to the floor.]

ASTYNAX: There are particles of light.
Look at the particles of light.
[points]
I can see them.

SIREN: [weeping] Those particles of light
came from the collision of his past into his present.
There are also particles of the night.

[There is weeping.]

ASYTNAX: At last I see your hand and face clearly, Ulysses.
I am no longer afraid of you.

I no longer hide from you.
You have come to be with me.
You have come willingly.

ULYSSES: I embrace all of you
  for all of you are parts of me,
  parts I have lost,
  parts I have killed,
  parts that find me in the darkest night of my soul.

  It is through my death that I embrace you.
  I should have been a balanced and wise man
  and embraced you in my life
  and kept all of you alive.

  It is through my embrace of you,
  through my death,
  you release me, and I release you.

  We are no longer bound to each other,
  we no longer seek each other out,
  we no longer weep for each other.

  We have undone the knot
  that has kept us bound and haunted to each other.

SIREN: No, no! Ulysses, don't leave!
  Don't leave me!
  I won't be able to reach you!
  Who will listen to my song?
  No! No!

PENELOPE: Ulysses, my love,
  you have cut the thread.
  The knife and law of the unseen
  has cut the thread to your life.
  You have taken another journey;
  I cannot follow.

Haunt me, follow me,
give me no peace or rest.
Be with me.

Curse me, bless me with your tears.

ULYSSES: My darling, you are so lovely.
Your eyes reveal the promise of dawn
and I have so much growing life around me.
Here the thread quivers and breaks and you cannot follow.
There are many in the room
and all seek me.

SIREN: Ulysses, I cannot reach your hand!
Swim to me!
Swim to the sea!

VOICES TOGETHER: Ulysses,
are you ready for your arrival?
Are you ready for your departure?
The world that you burned,
the world that you have saved,
will claim you, will consume you.

You wanted it this way.
The unspoken laws of the universe want it this way.
You have fallen in this battle.
The spear that is made from the bone of a sting ray
will pierce your heart.
Are you ready for your departure?

PENELOPE: My love.

ULYSSES: I seek you all.
I seek you all.

I embrace you all.
I am ready for my departure.

PENELOPE: Whisper to me. I am being engulfed by darkness.
 The sun has gone from my world.
 My love, I cannot bear to lose you for an eternity.
 Take me with you.

ULYSSES: I am taking you with me
 and you are keeping me with you.
 We suffer from a tension and suspension,
 for the finite is in the infinite,
 and the infinite in the finite.
 We have found our home in each other's hearts.
 This is how we keep each other alive.
 This is how we keep our love alive.
 When a bird and a fish fall in love, where do they live?

PENELOPE: In each other's hearts,
 my love, my life.

ULYSSES: We are the bird and the fish.
 Look for me in the sea, in the sky, in your heart.
 I live inside you now.

PENELOPE: My love, you have become more powerful,
 for now I have our youth,
 our life together and your death together.
 You live inside of me
 and that has made you more intense and alive in me.
 I have known love, and therefore,
 how can this love ever die?
 It continues in a different shape or form.
 It continues,
 the seed continues.

SIREN: Kiss me, Ulysses.

ASTYNAX: Kiss me, Ulysses.

DESTINY: Seal your destiny.
 Die well, Ulysses.

SIREN: Ulysses, you never told man the secret of the siren's song.
    It is the opening of a man's heart
    to reveal either the emptiness or fullness,
    and how much truth can you bear?

SIREN/ASTYNAX/ANDROMACHE/

DESTINY: [*together in voice and thoughts*] Do you see him?
    My eyes cannot follow him
    He has gone beyond the abyss and beyond separation.

    Did you know him?
    Did you love him?
    Will you remember him?

    It is in the last moments of life that a man sees—
    truly sees—
    the purpose of life,
    the mystery of death,
    truly sees, with the eyes of his soul,
    the beauty, miracle, and wonders of the world.
    These things that he did not really see while alive.

    It is at this time that trees, flowers, and mountains,
    rivers, birds, and the sunrise and sunset return
    and envelop all his senses.

    It is upon our death that the world and
    life becomes precious and lasting to us.

                [*There is weeping. The stage is in total darkness.*]

ACT IX
I AM READY FOR MY DEPARTURE

Colours of Sunrise

[*In this section of PENELOPE'S dialogue with herself and the reader, we are once again returned to the secret chambers: "in my beginning is my ending" and "in my ending is my beginning."*44

PENELOPE has come full circle, and this is her life message and thoughts on all the defeats and joys she has experienced in living with and without Ulysses, her thoughts on the purpose and meaning in life, and her thoughts about her departure from the audience's life.

It is the beginning of a new day. All the struggles have been fought and PENELOPE has multiplied in emotions and spirituality and intellect, and she knows her place in her life and the world.

The lights start to come on to create a Dawn. (The play begins with night and it ends with dawn.)

PENELOPE is standing, facing the audience, holding her sword upwards. She is standing by the sea.]

PENELOPE: I am ready for my departure.
    Has my life and journey brought you sadness?
    Devotion and belief
    that our love will continue in the world?
    There is no world without the making of love
    over and over again.

YOUNG PENELOPE: I took the journey.
    I travelled on the journey of life.
    I was blessed and cursed.

I planned and plotted to remain alive—
not surviving like animals
but alive, with imagination, vision, and dream.

BOTH: I am ready for my departure.

PENELOPE: I go from life to life
  and I am ready to continue,
  to continue, to continue.
  I am ready to eat away at eternity with the tiniest of shells.

YOUNG PENELOPE: Hail to you, my love!

PENELOPE: My brother, my comrade, my lover.

BOTH: You are welcome, whoever you are.

PENELOPE: Have you seen Ulysses?

YOUNG PENELOPE: Does he send a message with you?

PENELOPE: I have lived in exile among the dead, the living, the sirens,
  and the birds.

BOTH: They have chosen me
  and I embrace them as my home.

YOUNG PENELOPE: Ulysses was a wild bird.

PENELOPE: Ulysses was the salt in my journey,
  the sea I swam in and on.
  I am departing at the Dawn of the world—
  your world, my world, their world, our world,
  so many worlds,
  and we thought there was only ours.
  The world that makes and breaks
  and remakes itself over and over again.

BOTH: The "eternal recurrence,"[45]
 the eternal making of the world,
 over and over again.

PENELOPE: I want a universe for you where nothing dies.

YOUNG PENELOPE: Is there such a universe?

PENELOPE: A universe where nothing dies
 is where death is in life and life in death.
 Both are different births and endings;
 therefore, we go from life to life
 where you make the world over and over again
 in the image of deep longing,
 deep searching,
 deep seeking,
 deep surrendering,
 in the image of deep love.

YOUNG PENELOPE: I have whispered and shouted the eternal code
 of the beloved and the lover of the earth.

BOTH: For all I know is from this earth, this moment,
 as if time does not exist—it is an illusion.
 I am not concerned by time,
 although when I have transformed,
 this time as I know it
 will not exist for me.
 It will still continue to exist for others,
 but I would have changed into something else,
 something I do not recognise in this time,
 as the caterpillar does not recognise the butterfly,
 nor does it know it is the same entity.
 Time has been distant from me.

 Life has been the one that I have chased after.
 It is life that has been my siren:
 connecting me, disconnecting me, playing with me,

149

tormenting me, offering me, removing from me,
taking from me, giving to me, and always laughing:
"This is not the end between you and me!"

This universe does not die. It multiplies.
It scatters its seeds into the next generation.
It changes and transforms the previous generations,
as all layers of generations are suspended and quivering
above and below each other—
the world makes itself over and over again.

BOTH: Keep loving the earth; keep devoted
    to the life you are in.
    Do not take the face of another.
    Remain true to yourself.

YOUNG PENELOPE: And now that you are leaving,
    take some part of me with you into the light.
    I have touched parts
    of your unspoken world.
    We are taught not to share our vulnerabilities,
    our sensitivities, our visions,
    and therefore this becomes the unspoken world of another,
    the sunken world.
    How can you live a full life with a full heart—
    with a sunken vision?
    Vision is meant to be lived and shared, not drowned
    where even the mermaids lose their glory.

    I have travelled on the sea of life
    without maps and charts.
    I have lived the human adventure with a full heart.

PENELOPE: How does it stand here,
    above and below,
    backwards and forwards?

YOUNG PENELOPE: The relativity of time and travel
    from one place to the other,
    without even seeing movement,
    not a sound . . .
    You are pushed into the world
    and pulled without any warning, without any sound,
    back into metamorphosis—
    another birth.
    Without movement or wheels,
    without maps or charts,
    we find our way into the world
    and find our way into the next realm,
    the next birth.
    We find our arrival.
    We are there for our departure
    and know precisely where to be and where to go
    for our unknown destinations.

PENELOPE: Our arrival into life;
    our departure into the unknown.

YOUNG PENELOPE: Upon our arrival in life
    we are also entering the unknown,
    and yet we cling to this known
    as if it were the only life, the only experience
    that we will ever go through.

BOTH: Our lives are full of arrivals and departures.

PENELOPE: How does it stand here,
    that the wheels and trains and planes
    move without progress,
    and with fixed destinations?
    Where is the adventure
    if you know exactly where you are going to go,
    who you will be with,
    what you will wear,

how you will look,
and how you will act.
Where is the adventure
in such a controlled destination?

BOTH: We are all navigators in the sea of life.
"And there is the sea and who will drink it dry?"[46]

YOUNG PENELOPE: Man, among all creatures,
is the most desirable to me.

BOTH: The most frightening.

PENELOPE: The one that knows of the progress and stages of life,
the cycle of birth and death,
and still pretends that these laws do not apply to him.

YOUNG PENELOPE: The most lovable
and by far the most desirable one.

PENELOPE: It is strange, how when we are older,
words that we have used when we were younger
come back to haunt us.

BOTH: Man has the capacity to create, to make, to invent,
to heal, to love, to harvest peace and prosperity to all.

PENELOPE: How does one know
if one loves from their soul,
from their vision,
from the depths and sleep of eternity?

YOUNG PENELOPE: They make fire in the heart of others.
They make fire for us to see each other.
They make fire and play around it like young children.
They make fire
and give light from their struggle in life and with life.
This fire, this heat and light,
connects us to our lives and to the lives of others.

We become both alive in life and alive in death.
This is what they mean by not being separated by death,
and a love going beyond death.

PENELOPE: It is this fire in the heart, in the spirit of man
    that multiplies;
    it generates and consumes the fire giver
    and the fire taker.
    These are the seeds from eternity
    that we pass on to each other.

YOUNG PENELOPE: We pass the seed of love,
    the seed of fire,
    the seed of eternity,
    the seed of "memory" to each other.
    We infect and affect each other.

PENELOPE: What happens to those
    who are seed carriers of memory and fire?

YOUNG PENELOPE: We bury them in the ground
    so that they can grow and we can all eat from their fruit.
    They let us bury them into the ground.
    Surely such evolved people would know
    that if they exposed too much fire or light
    others who do not want to be seen or exposed
    would come to put the fire out, to put them into the ground—
    and they still do it, not out of spite or defiance
    but out of love.

PENELOPE: Thank goodness we cannot contain
    the wild bird's vision
    or the song of the siren.
    "It is the madmen and children
    who keep the fires burning."[47]

YOUNG PENELOPE: What would happen to the world
    if we removed the seed carriers from every generation?

What would happen
if we cut down the trees in the soul?

BOTH: We would be engulfed in total darkness.

PENELOPE: The seed carriers
      postulate and bury unseen seeds
      in the journey of the human heart
      to promote justice and peace,
      to abolish exploitation of others,
      to abolish wars,
      to increase the ever-threatened dignity and life of man.

      It is love that reaches us
      from the shores of the invisible and the visible,
      like the siren's song
      echoing a message that cannot be heard
      in human voice
      that reaches us—from where?

YOUNG PENELOPE: From the struggles and sacrifices of our lives,
      from those we kept afloat in life,
      from those who keep us afloat from the other shore,
      from the rivers of human tears.

BOTH: The aching longing.
      The shores that we reach and cannot reach.
      The measureless human tears.

PENELOPE: We dream of voyages through our connection
      to the seeds of longing.
      We create and grieve through the fire of our love,
      the fire in our being.
      We arrive and depart with the light,
      with the burning in our soul
      that gives us direction and guidance.

BOTH: Love is in us or nowhere.
    Humanity is in us or nowhere.
    Kindness is in us or nowhere.
    "Eternity is in us or nowhere."[48]

PENELOPE: Do you have regrets?

YOUNG PENELOPE: And would you change anything
    if you could be taken forward
    and backward into your life?

BOTH: Would you change anything at all?
    Would you offer your love to a stranger?
    Would you feed and clothe a stranger,
    wanting and seeking nothing in return?

PENELOPE: I do not have any regrets
    upon the journey I have taken,
    the love that I have shared,
    the love that was stolen and hidden from me,
    the long years of solitude
    in which I found myself and my life.

YOUNG PENELOPE: I chose to live in the forest
    and now I have returned to the sea.
    I have multiplied as all fish returning home to the sea—
    and so full of seed.

PENELOPE: I have come to an end.
    If someone could continue where I have stopped
    And there above me and below me,
    my life waves to me for recognition.

YOUNG PENELOPE: For life chose me
    and I choose life over and over again.

PENELOPE: I chose the road that took me away from
    prestige, recognition, and power—
    I chose freedom.

YOUNG PENELOPE: How do you bury a man who has loved?

PENELOPE: How do you bury a man who has loved?
    can it be that the man who does not love
    is buried while he is alive, in forgetfulness,
    and he is a sleepwalker in his life?

YOUNG PENELOPE: And upon his physical death,
    he disappears into the void of nothingness
    as if he had never been born.

BOTH: Can it be that the man
    who loves the kindred and the stranger never dies?
    For we bury him in our mind, in our heart.
    We pass him on as seeds for the next generation to eat from.

PENELOPE: This man lives in the fire of our soul and spirit.
    These type of seeds stay in our digestion
    to stir us up:
    into our minds to annoy us,
    into our vision to make us weep,
    into the darkest night of our soul to give us hope.

BOTH: With deep tenderness and longing
    to speak with him once again . . .

YOUNG PENELOPE: I see Ulysses in all the faces of the world.

PENELOPE: Our love goes above and below
    the union and mating of man and woman.
    Our love is fused and interwoven
    with the thread and tensions of seed carriers
    —the light givers.

BOTH: I came here to love, not to hate.[49]

PENELOPE: Have I gone too far?
    Will the hunters catch me?
    Will they throw their nets over me

and drag me in like a creature
freshly caught from the sea or from the forest?

YOUNG PENELOPE: I think they have declared me mad,
　　which is better than being declared dead,
　　for the mad can speak with the dead,
　　for the mad can speak for the dead and the living.

PENELOPE: The armies of those whom I love
　　consume me and engulf me.

YOUNG PENELOPE: And I engulf them.

PENELOPE: They will not let me pass until I go with them . . .

YOUNG PENELOPE: Respond to them . . .

BOTH: And I charge full with all my force . . . !

PENELOPE: Did you see the seeds of eternity fly into the sky?
　　And as they fall, young children,
　　angels and tormented devils
　　put them quietly under their tongues . . .

BOTH: To keep them safe, so that they can chew on them
　　on a dark, lonely night.

PENELOPE: To keep for when there is a crisis.
　　When it becomes dark and no light can be seen
　　they will feed on the ancestor's seeds.
　　They will feed on the fire of others.
　　They will feed on the soul that has been left here for them.

BOTH: Now to be sure,
　　it seems internally and externally dark.

PENELOPE: So lonely and formless.

YOUNG PENELOPE: There is nothing to fear.
　　Love does not enter through

the expected doors and windows.

PENELOPE: Love is a rebel. Love comes to us.
　　　It reaches us through illegal paths and ways.
　　　It cannot be called love
　　　if it is domesticated, confined, planned.
　　　It cannot be love if it seeks rewards.
　　　This gesture is an illusion of love.

　　　Do you want to remain the same?

　　　No, I go from life to life,
　　　eating away at my life and eternity with a tiny sea shell

YOUNG PENELOPE: We became a tree in the world,
　　　collecting dreams from the sky
　　　and keeping the earth together.

BOTH: Such a love comes through the back door
　　　and challenges us to pull the whole house down.

YOUNG PENELOPE: So that we can see each other.

PENELOPE: So we can create a universe that does not die—

　　　and above all, and below all things
　　　(forgotten, buried, or stolen)—
　　　make decisions we can live with for the rest of our lives.

BOTH: Make decisions that give life.

PENELOPE: Then we can see each other
　　　without shame or fear,
　　　without power or domination.

BOTH: We will see each other.

PENELOPE: In the battle of my life
　　　the lessons of war
　　　are that we must fight

to keep something alive—

to keep love alive.

Of all the fires of the heart
love is the only inexhaustible one:
it unites both the kindred and the stranger;
it unites both life and death.

[PENELOPE's dialogue ends with *the celebration of a coming dawn*]

[MUSIC LYRICS: "If we want the sun to return
we have much work and much struggle
as a united people," "A Solitary Swallow," by Odysseus Elytis]

THE END

SOME SMALL SEEDS OF GRATITUDE FROM THE JOURNEY

I thank you for waiting for me.

I thank you for travelling this journey with me.

As a poet, I have struggled with the idea of taking pictures, writing the vision down, writing about the struggle and the discoveries of the human heart that is in love with the seeking and searching Psyche.

Plato believed a person consisted of three parts:

- the mind, the intellect
- the heart, the passions
- the instincts, the sexual drives

The guidance for our human journey comes from the heart: it guides the mind to merge reason with compassion and justice—not just intellectual rationalism, a form of self-serving agenda also known as sophistry.

Plato also believed that the drives need to have the heart to guide them; otherwise, the "dark horse," as he wrote, would turn the person into a brute. It is the heart that is the centre of all life, and Plato believed the centre of the person needed to guide both the mind and the drives. Lacking this guidance, the person would be either indifferent to others or a savage.

So it has been for me. I have travelled into the journey of the human heart, and I realised there was another part to this—the unison with Psyche. It is Psyche that urges us on to travel the road of the humane, seeking the path within the labyrinth of our human journey and the miracle of others who travel beside us, before us, after us, and those that live with us now.

Psyche travels in dark passages. All things grow from the fertility of darkness, and there is no rest for one who follows the path of Psyche. It is her purpose to challenge us so that we find the seeds from the infinite and then she insists that we bring these seeds of humanity into the light for all others to see, share and feed on.

Solomos wrote, "The eyes of my psyche are always awake; they never sleep— always awake."

Heraclitus knew of these uncharted and unmapped journeys of the human Psyche when he wrote

"You could not reach
the ends of the Psyche
though, you want the whole
Way; so deep is its nature"

One creates from raw materials when one is on this journey: raw materials as they come from the unknown and the unexplored—the dream world, as it is known in some cultures. In others it is the quest and vision. In others, compassionate and humane creativity. The creator of such a world has to be both mother and father in this creative and dangerous journey—dangerous because the world may reject this creator for their findings and the gifts they make through the expression of their art.

But for an artist not to take this journey or this risk would only destroy them from the inside, as they have abandoned all they see, worship, connect to, struggle with, and deeply love.

How does one surrender the journey of their heart and psyche to the stranger and the kindred?

With humility and gratitude.

As a writer I express my journey through masks. Penelope and Ulysses are such masks. Through these masks I am creating other people to speak for me the many tensions and dimensions, the search within the labyrinth of human passions, of human betrayal, of human longing, of human compassion, of human struggle and surrender. One creates a whole world: the map of their soul and human journey. This is done from the deepest affection for others and our world—as Yannis Ritsos writes, "so we can understand each other."

All our arts and all our lasting artists expose us to deep humanity and longing for a better life and a better world for all of us.

In the culture I shared in my first eight years, I was taught by my illiterate grandmother that having a vision, being creative, and being a seeker of truth and beauty[50] was a natural state of being, and anyone who became lazy and indifferent to the struggle of truth and beauty (which we call art) was, by nature and destiny, to suffer atrophy. In this remote part of the world and culture, art was making your life a work of art. We did not have an academic language to tell us what art was because we lived in a seeking, searching, creative way. In my life later life, in the world of academia, I learned that the "academic is fragile like crystal"[51] and if one is an "artist" one must be elite and serious.

I decided to stay with the illiterate story teller, and when she could not tell me any more stories, I decided to educate myself so that I could read the messages that my family has left for me, to sustain me, to comfort me, to challenge me, and to inspire me.

Therefore I certainly do not explore, invent, and write to achieve recognition and fame: it is natural to me to travel into the world of imagination (not to be confused with fantasy), vision, and intuition.

When I was a child I used to listen to the trees: they breathe and some actually move. I learned to love the unnamed, the unseen, the untouched, and the unfound. I could not follow the path of others, nor could I lead others to my path. I knew from an early age about the "creative quick."[52]

Now that you are leaving, now that the day of payment
dawns, now that no one knows
whom he will kill and how he will die
take with you the boy who saw the light
under the leaves of that plane tree
and teach him to study the trees.[53]

I came into my life late, and I will never leave it again.

I have struggled with the idea and praxis of going public, putting my vision on paper and offering it to both kindred and the stranger. I have hidden my work and my creative thoughts and worlds from others, simply because I do not want to be confined or formulated, "and when I am formulated ... [and] pinned ... how should I begin to spit out ... my days?"[54]

The other tension in me is that I do not desire to lead, I simply desire to share and to return to my solitude.

Through this journey that I have shared, I learned some things about sharing that I had forgotten.

If I do not give myself permission to share this with others, my avoidance and silence would be an admission that the sensitive and intelligent do not belong here; in truth, we have a great need for the sensitive, compassionate, and intelligent in our life and world.

Where would I be if my humankind family had not left their song for me to share, challenge, inspire me, and keep my soul warm in the darkest night?

This type of invention and exploration is a process of finding inner worlds that so many fear to travel in or speak about, the inner worlds that connect us to life, others, the past, present, and future, the inner voice of "self-ownership."[55]

Within this struggle and inspiration I discovered that if I did not share my song with others then I would not be worthy of what my navigating ancestors have offered me freely. I also discovered that unless I was willing to share this vision, it lacked the affirmation of blood, my devotion and commitment to it. Although I love the songs that others have left for me, this is my song, and in humility and gratitude I say thank you to them, and you, for staying, for seeing, for exploring what I invented and created.

Thank you for allowing me the gift to share this creativity with you.

Thank you for teaching me to offer my work.

I thank those that have waited for me:

the past generations and navigators;
those that are with me now;
and those that will wait for me when they arrive later.

All that has been written is from

Myth
Fact
and Nonsense.

Endnotes

1 The Bible, Deuteronomy 8: 2-3 (King James Version)
2 Nietzsche, Friedrich. *The Gay Science*, trans. Walter Kaufmann. New York: Vintage Books, 1974, § 276, p. 223.
3 Ritsos, Yannis. From *The Fourth Dimension: Selected Poems of Yannis Ritsos*, transl. *Rae Dalven*. Godine, 1977.
4 Miller, Alice. "The Essential Role of an Enlightened Witness in Society", 1 January, 1997. From: *http://www.alice-miller.com*
5 "Socrates said he was not an Athenian or a Greek, but a citizen of the world". Plutarch (Greek essayist and biographer, A.D. 46-A.D. 120), "Of Banishment".
6 The epitaph on the grave of Nikos Kazantzakis.
7 "Of all that is written, I love only what a person hath written with his blood, and thou will find that blood is spirit". Nietzsche, Friedrich. *Thus Spake Zarathustra, translated by Thomas Common*. The Pennsylvania State University, 1999.
8 Kierkegaard, Soren, and Rohde, Peter P, *The diary of Soren Kierkegaard / translated from the Danish by Gerda M. Anderson; edited by Peter P. Rohde Owen*, London, 1960.
9 "The Love Song of J. Alfred Prufrock", from: Eliot, Thomas Stearns. *Prufrock and Other Observations*. From Poems. New York: A.A. Knopf, 1920; Bartleby. com, 2011.
10 "Do not go gentle into that Good Night". Thomas, Dylan, and Jones, Daniel, *The poems of Dylan Thomas/edited with an introduction and notes by Daniel Jones*, New York: New Directions Pub. Corp., 1971.
11 "Ode to a Grecian Urn". Keats, John. *Poetical Works*, London: Macmillan, 1884; Bartleby.com, 1999.
12 Plato. and Cary, Henry. and Burges, George. and Davis, Henry. *The works of Plato*. London, New York: G. Bell & sons, , 1891.
13 As above.
14 "Socrates said he was not an Athenian or a Greek, but a citizen of the world". Plutarch (Greek essayist and biographer, A.D. 46-A.D. 120), "Of Banishment".
15 Elytis, Odysseus. *What I love: Selected Poems of Odysseus Elytis, translated by Olga Broumas*, Copper Canyon Press, 1986.
16 Reed, Henry. "Unarmed Combat." New Statesman and Nation 29, no. 740 (28 April 1945): 271.
17 Zenovia. *Penelope*, work in progress.

18 Shakespeare, William, and Hunter, G. K. *King Lear/William Shakespeare; edited by G.K.* Hunter. Harmondsworth: Penguin, 1972.

19 Aeschylus, and Fagles, Robert, *The Oresteia: Agamemnon; The Libation Bearers; The Eumenides; translated by Robert Fagles;* London: Penguin Books, 1977.

20 As above.

21 As above.

22 As above.

23 Shakespeare, William. Much ado about nothing Penguin, London : 1954

24 Nietzsche, Friedrich. *Thus Spake Zarathustra, translated by Thomas Common.* The Pennsylvania State University, 1999.

25 Aeschylus, *Oresteia*, and William Shakespeare, *Macbeth*

26 Euripides, *The Trojan Women*

27 Nietzsche, Friedrich. *Thus Spake Zarathustra, translated by Thomas Common.* The Pennsylvania State University, 1999.

28 Shakespeare, William. and Davidson, Ric. *Shakespeare Macbeth / edited by Ric Davidson.* Avalon Beach, NSW: Lion Island, 2003.

29 Aeschylus, and Fagles, Robert, *The Oresteia: Agamemnon; The Libation Bearers; The Eumenides; translated by Robert Fagles;* London: Penguin Books, 1977.

30 Aeschylus, *Oresteia*, and William Shakespeare, *Macbeth*.

31 Shakespeare, William. and Davidson, Ric. *Shakespeare Macbeth / edited by Ric Davidson.* Avalon Beach, NSW: Lion Island, 2003.

32 Aeschylus, and Fagles, Robert, *The Oresteia: Agamemnon; The Libation Bearers; The Eumenides; translated by Robert Fagles;* London: Penguin Books, 1977.

33 As above.

34 As above.

35 As above.

36 Orwell, George. "Politics and the English Language". GB, London: Horizon, 1946.

37 Dante Alighieri. and Longfellow, Henry Wadsworth. *The Divine comedy of Dante Alighieri. Inferno.* London: Routledge and sons, 1867.

38 Gatsos. Nikos. *Amorgos.* translated by Sally Purcell. 1980; London: Anvil Press Poetry, 1998.

39 Agathon, from Aristotle. and Thomson, J. A. K. *The ethics of Aristotle : the Nicomachean ethics/translated by J.A.K.* London: *Thomson* Allen & Unwin, 1953.

40 Zarathustra, the philosopher, believed that a man should focus on doing more good when alive and in bloom, for he believed that upon death, all his good deeds reveal themselves to him and make the transition of light. Similarly, if a man has committed crimes of the blood and the destruction of others, these deeds also come to life upon one's deathbed, and they become demons. Zarathustra

advised that we remain focused in our lives, to know the connections we have with others, to make sure that we do more good to assist others and ourselves in our human journey, to assist us to have a "good death" as we have a good life—as the classical philosophers spoke about.

41 Dante Alighieri. and Longfellow, Henry Wadsworth. *The Divine comedy of Dante Alighieri. Inferno.* London: Routledge and sons, 1867.

42 Agathon, from Aristotle. and Thomson, J. A. K. *The ethics of Aristotle : the Nicomachean ethics/translated by J.A.K.* London: *Thomson* Allen & Unwin, 1953.

43 Whitman, Walt. and Murphy, Francis. *The complete poems/Walt Whitman; edited by Francis Murphy.* Harmondsworth: Penguin Education, 1975.

44 "East Coker". From Eliot, T. S. *Four quartets/T.S. Eliot.* New York: Harcourt Brace, 1943.

45 Nietzsche, Friedrich. *Thus Spake Zarathustra, translated by Thomas Common.* The Pennsylvania State University, 1999.

46 Aeschylus, and Fagles, Robert, *The Oresteia: Agamemnon; The Libation Bearers; The Eumenides; translated by Robert Fagles;* London: Penguin Books, 1977.

47 Seferis, George. *Complete Poems* trans. Edmund Keeley and Philip Sherrard. London: Anvil Press Poetry, 1995.

48 Novalis. and Hope, M. J. and Just, Coelest August. *Novalis (Friedrich von Hardenberg): his life, thoughts and works/edited and translated by M.J.* London: *Hope* Stott, 1891.

49 Sophocles. and Watling, E. F. and Sophocles. and Sophocles. and Sophocles. *The Theban plays: King Oedipus, Oedipus at Colonus, Antigone/Sophocles ; translated by E.F. Watling.* Harmondsworth, Middlesex: Penguin Books, 1947.

50 "Beauty is truth, and truth beauty. That is all ye know on earth and all ye need to know." From Keats, John, "Ode to a Grecian Urn". From: Quiller-Couch, Arthur Thomas, Sir. *The Oxford Book of English Verse.* Oxford: Clarendon, 1919; Bartleby.com, 1999.

51 Chekhov, Anton, *Letters on the Short Story, the Drama and other Literary Topics,* selected and edited by Louis S. Friedland. New York: Minton, Balch & Co., 1924.

52 Lawrence, D. H., "The poetry of the present". From: www.poetryfoundation. org/learning/essay/237874

53 Seferis, George, and Walton, Mary Cooper. *Mythistorema and Gymnopaidia/ George Seferis; with translation by Mary Cooper Walton.* Athens, Greece: Lycabettus Press, 1977.

54 "The Love Song of J. Alfred Prufrock", from: Eliot, Thomas Stearns. *Prufrock and Other Observations.* From Poems. New York: A.A. Knopf, 1920; Bartleby. com, 2011.

55 Nietzsche, Friedrich. *Thus Spake Zarathustra, translated by Thomas Common.* The Pennsylvania State University, 1999.

Printed in the United States
by Baker & Taylor Publisher Services